Table of Con

I'm Scarlett!

Welcome Aboard the Baking Express!

We're chuffed to have you join us on this fantastic journey into the world of quick and delicious treats, perfect for busy teenagers like you!

Whether you're a complete baking novice or a budding pastry chef, this book is packed with scrumptious recipes, helpful tips, and fun activities designed to suit your fast-paced lifestyle.

Throughout this guide, we'll be sharing a delightful array of recipes, from speedy sweets like cookies and brownies to no-bake desserts that will have you whipping up indulgent treats in a jiffy.

But that's not all! We'll also be covering essential baking skills, time-saving hacks, and creative decorating ideas that will help you wow your family and mates alike.

Let's get baking!

With the Baking Express as your guide, you'll soon discover the joy and satisfaction that comes from creating quick, delicious, and homemade treats.

In addition to providing you with mouth-watering recipes and valuable techniques, we understand the importance of well-being and self-care.

That's why we've included a special chapter on baking as a way to beat exam stress, offering so othing recipes and mindful baking activities that can help you unwind and find comfort during high-pressure moments.

So, pop on your apron, preheat the oven, and get ready to embark on a fantastic baking adventure!

Speedy Sweets
Quick and Easy Cookie Recipes

Welcome to the first stop on our Baking Express journey!

In this chapter, we'll be diving into the delightful world of cookies. Whether you fancy something classic like a chocolate chip cookie or a biscuit with a bit more oomph, you'll find a splendid selection of quick and easy recipes to satisfy your sweet tooth.

So, let's crack on and explore the scrumptious world of speedy sweets!

Classic Chocolate Chip Cookies

🕐 **15 minutes**

Indulge in the classic goodness of freshly baked chocolate chip cookies with this easy recipe. Simple ingredients, quick preparation, and delicious results guaranteed!

Ingredients

225g unsalted butter, softened
150g granulated sugar
160g light brown sugar
2 large eggs
1 tsp vanilla extract
375g plain flour
1 tsp baking soda
1/2 tsp salt
200g milk, dark or semi-sweet chocolate chips

Method

- Preheat your oven to 190°C (170°C fan/gas mark 5) and line two baking trays with baking parchment.
- In a large mixing bowl, cream together the softened butter, granulated sugar, and light brown sugar until smooth.
- Beat in the eggs one at a time, then stir in the vanilla extract.
- In a separate bowl, whisk together the plain flour, baking soda, and salt. Gradually add the dry ingredients to the wet ingredients, mixing until just combined.
- Fold in the chocolate chips.
- Drop rounded tablespoonfuls of dough onto the prepared baking trays, spacing them about 5cm apart.
- Bake for 8-10 minutes or until lightly golden around the edges. Let the cookies cool on the trays for a few minutes before transferring them to a wire rack to cool completely.

Oatmeal Raisin Delights

🕐 **15 minutes**

Enjoy a wholesome twist on the traditional oatmeal cookie with this recipe for Oatmeal Raisin Delights. Soft, chewy, and packed with flavor, these cookies are perfect for any occasion.

Ingredients

150g unsalted butter, softened
100g granulated sugar
100g light brown sugar
2 large eggs
1 tsp vanilla extract
190g plain flour
1/2 tsp baking soda
1/2 tsp salt
1 tsp ground cinnamon
240g rolled oats
200g raisins

Method

- Preheat your oven to 180°C (160°C fan/gas mark 4) and line two baking trays with baking parchment.
- In a large mixing bowl, cream together the softened butter, granulated sugar, and light brown sugar until smooth.
- Beat in the eggs one at a time, then stir in the vanilla extract.
- In a separate bowl, whisk together the plain flour, baking soda, salt, and ground cinnamon. Gradually add the dry ingredients to the wet ingredients, mixing until just combined.
- Stir in the rolled oats and raisins.
- Drop rounded tablespoonfuls of dough onto the prepared baking trays, spacing them about 5cm apart.
- Bake for 10-12 minutes or until the edges are lightly golden. Let the cookies cool on the trays for a few minutes before transferring them to a wire rack to cool completely.

Marvellous Macaroons

🕐 **20 minutes**

Transport yourself to a French patisserie with this recipe for Marvellous Macaroons. These delicate treats are surprisingly easy to make and will impress any dessert lover.

Ingredients

200g desiccated coconut
150g granulated sugar
2 large egg whites
1 tsp vanilla extract
Pinch of salt

Method

- Preheat your oven to 160°C (140°C fan/gas mark 3) and line two baking trays with baking parchment.
- In a large mixing bowl, combine the desiccated coconut and granulated sugar.
- In a separate bowl, whisk the egg whites, vanilla extract, and salt until frothy.
- Fold the egg white mixture into the coconut mixture until well combined.
- Drop rounded tablespoonfuls of the mixture onto the prepared baking trays, spacing them about 5cm apart.
- Bake for 15-20 minutes or until the macaroons are lightly golden.
- Let the macaroons cool on the trays for a few minutes before transferring them to a wire rack to cool completely.

Peanut Butter Perfection

🕐 **15 minutes**

Satisfy your peanut butter cravings with these Peanut Butter Perfection Biscuits. Soft, chewy, and packed with nutty flavour, these biscuits are perfect for breakfast, snack, or dessert.

Ingredients

250g smooth peanut butter
150g granulated sugar
1 large egg
1 tsp baking soda
1/2 tsp vanilla extract

Method

- Preheat your oven to 180°C (160°C fan/gas mark 4) and line two baking trays with baking parchment.
- In a large mixing bowl, combine the peanut butter, granulated sugar, egg, baking soda, and vanilla extract until well mixed.
- Drop rounded tablespoonfuls of dough onto the prepared baking trays, spacing them about 5cm apart. Flatten each cookie slightly with a fork, creating a criss-cross pattern.
- Bake for 8-10 minutes or until the edges are set. Let the cookies cool on the trays for a few minutes before transferring them to a wire rack to cool completely.

Lovely Lemon Shortbread

🕐 **20 minutes**

Elevate your cookie game with this recipe for Lemon Shortbread. Rich, buttery, and infused with zesty lemon flavour, these cookies are a refreshing twist on a classic treat.

Ingredients

225g unsalted butter, softened
100g granulated sugar
Zest of 1 lemon
1/2 tsp vanilla extract
260g plain flour
1/4 tsp salt

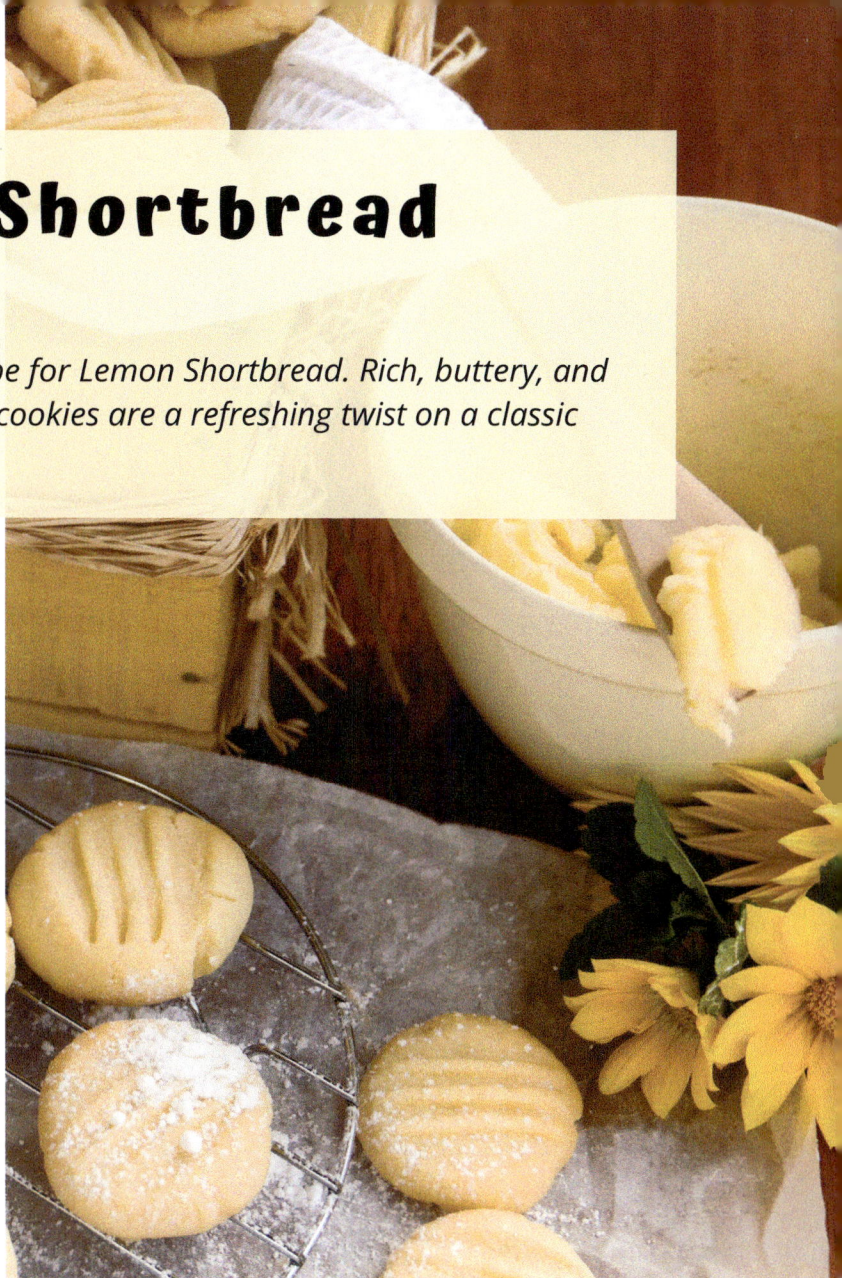

Method

- Preheat your oven to 160°C (140°C fan/gas mark 3) and line two baking trays with baking parchment.
- In a large mixing bowl, cream together the softened butter, granulated sugar, and lemon zest until smooth. Stir in the vanilla extract.
- Gradually add the plain flour and salt to the wet ingredients, mixing until just combined.
- Roll the dough out to about 0.5cm thickness on a lightly floured surface. Use a cookie cutter to cut out shapes, and place them on the prepared baking trays.
- Bake for 12-15 minutes or until the edges are lightly golden. Let the cookies cool on the trays for a few minutes before transferring them to a wire rack to cool completely.

Double Chocolate Chunkies

🕐 **20 minutes**

Chocolate Chunkies are the ultimate chocolate lover's dream. These soft and chewy cookies are packed with both semisweet and white chocolate chunks for a decadent treat that's hard to resist.

Ingredients

190g all-purpose flour
35g unsweetened cocoa powder
1 teaspoon baking powder
1/2 teaspoon baking soda
1/4 teaspoon salt
115g unsalted butter, softened
100g granulated sugar
100g brown sugar
2 large eggs
1 teaspoon vanilla extract
180g semisweet chocolate chunks
90g white/dark chocolate chunks

Method

- Preheat the oven to 160°C (fan)/180°C (conventional)/gas mark 4 and line a baking sheet with parchment paper.
- In a medium bowl, whisk together the flour, cocoa powder, baking powder, baking soda, and salt.
- In a large bowl, beat the butter, granulated sugar, and brown sugar together until light and fluffy.
- Add the eggs, one at a time, beating well after each addition.
- Stir in the vanilla extract.
- Gradually add the dry ingredients to the wet ingredients, mixing until just combined.
- Stir in the chocolate chunks.
- Using a cookie scoop or spoon, drop the dough onto the prepared baking sheet, spacing them about 5cm apart.
- Bake for 12-15 minutes, or until the edges are set and the centers are still slightly soft.
- Let the cookies cool on the baking sheet for 5 minutes, then transfer them to a wire rack to cool completely.

Spiced Ginger Snaps

🕐 **15 minutes**

Spiced ginger snaps are a classic holiday treat that pack a punch of warm, cozy flavours. These crispy, spicy cookies are perfect for snacking on with a cup of tea or sharing with loved ones.

Ingredients

170g unsalted butter, softened
200g granulated sugar
1 large egg
80ml molasses
375g plain flour
2 tsp baking soda
1/2 tsp salt
1 tsp ground ginger
1 tsp ground cinnamon
1/2 tsp ground cloves
1/4 tsp ground nutmeg
Additional granulated sugar for rolling

Method

- Preheat your oven to 190°C (170°C fan/gas mark 5) and line two baking trays with baking parchment.
- In a large mixing bowl, cream together the softened butter and granulated sugar until smooth.
- Beat in the egg and molasses.
- In a separate bowl, whisk together the plain flour, baking soda, salt, ground ginger, ground cinnamon, ground cloves, and ground nutmeg. Gradually add the dry ingredients to the wet ingredients, mixing until just combined.
- Shape the dough into small balls and roll each ball in the additional granulated sugar. Place them on the prepared baking trays, spacing them about 5cm apart.
- Bake for 10-12 minutes or until the cookies are set and have a crackled appearance. Let the cookies cool on the trays for a few minutes before transferring them to a wire rack to cool completely.

Cranberry & White Chocolate Bites

🕐 **20 minutes**

These White Chocolate Cranberry Cookies are a delicious and indulgent treat that are perfect for any occasion. Made with soft, chewy cookie dough and loaded with chunks of white chocolate and tart dried cranberries, they're sure to satisfy any sweet tooth.

Ingredients

225g unsalted butter, softened

150g granulated sugar

160g light brown sugar

2 large eggs

1 tsp vanilla extract

375g plain flour

1 tsp baking soda

1/2 tsp salt

150g white chocolate, chopped

150g dried cranberries

Method

- Preheat your oven to 190°C (170°C fan/gas mark 5) and line two baking trays with baking parchment.
- In a large mixing bowl, cream together the softened butter, granulated sugar, and light brown sugar until smooth.
- Beat in the eggs one at a time, then stir in the vanilla extract.
- In a separate bowl, whisk together the plain flour, baking soda, and salt. Gradually add the dry ingredients to the wet ingredients, mixing until just combined.
- Fold in the chopped white chocolate and dried cranberries.
- Drop rounded tablespoonfuls of dough onto the prepared baking trays, spacing them about 5cm apart.
- Bake for 8-10 minutes or until lightly golden around the edges. Let the cookies cool on the trays for a few minutes before transferring them to a wire rack to cool completely.

No-Bake Energy Cookies

🕒 **5 minutes**

Wholesome and quick, No-Bake Energy Cookies are perfect for on-the-go snacking. Made with oats, peanut butter, honey, chocolate chips, nuts, and fruit for a healthy energy boost.

Ingredients

200g rolled oats
100g smooth peanut butter
80g honey
50g dark chocolate chips
50g chopped nuts (e.g., almonds, walnuts, or pecans)
50g dried fruit (e.g., raisins, cranberries, or chopped apricots)

Method

- In a large mixing bowl, combine the rolled oats, peanut butter, and honey.
- Mix well until fully combined.
- Fold in the dark chocolate chips, chopped nuts, and dried fruit.
- Line a baking tray with baking parchment.
- Using your hands, shape the mixture into small balls or flatten them into cookie shapes, or cut them into bars and place them on the prepared baking tray.
- Refrigerate the cookies for at least 30 minutes or until firm before enjoying them. Store any leftovers in an airtight container in the refrigerator.

Marvellous Muffins
Fast and Flavourful Bites for Breakfast

Welcome to the next stop on our Baking Express journey: The land of marvellous muffins! This chapter is dedicated to helping you create fast and flavourful bites that are perfect for breakfast, a mid-morning snack, or even dessert. Muffins are a versatile and convenient treat, and with the recipes we've got lined up, you'll never be short of tasty options. So, let's get started!

Banana Chocolate Chip Muffins

🕐 **15 minutes**

These banana chocolate chip muffins are the perfect way to start your day. Made with ripe bananas and loaded with milk, dark, or semi-sweet chocolate chips, they're a sweet and satisfying breakfast treat.

Ingredients

250g plain flour

150g granulated sugar

1/2 tsp salt

1/2 tsp baking powder

1/2 tsp bicarbonate of soda

1/4 tsp ground cinnamon

3 ripe bananas, mashed

75g vegetable oil

1 large egg

1 tsp vanilla extract

150g chocolate chips

Method

- Preheat your oven to 180°C (160°C fan/gas mark 4) and line a 12-cup muffin tin with paper cases.
- In a large mixing bowl, whisk together the plain flour, granulated sugar, salt, baking powder, bicarbonate of soda, and ground cinnamon.
- In a separate bowl, combine the mashed bananas, vegetable oil, egg, and vanilla extract.
- Fold the wet ingredients into the dry ingredients until just combined. Stir in the chocolate chips.
- Spoon the batter into the muffin cases, filling each about two-thirds full.
- Bake for 20-25 minutes, or until a toothpick inserted into the centre of a muffin comes out clean. Allow the muffins to cool in the tin for 5 minutes before transferring them to a wire rack to cool completely.

Blueberry Burst Muffins

🕐 **35 minutes**

This easy blueberry muffin recipe uses simple ingredients like flour, sugar, baking powder, eggs, and milk, combined with sweet, juicy blueberries. Perfect for breakfast or a snack, these muffins are light, fluffy, and bursting with flavour

Ingredients

375g plain flour
150g granulated sugar
1/2 tsp salt
3 tsp baking powder
240ml milk
120ml vegetable oil
2 large eggs
1 tsp vanilla extract
250g fresh or frozen blueberries

Method

- Preheat your oven to 200°C (180°C fan/gas mark 6) and line a 12-cup muffin tin with paper cases.
- In a large mixing bowl, whisk together the plain flour, granulated sugar, salt, and baking powder.
- In a separate bowl, whisk together the milk, vegetable oil, eggs, and vanilla extract.
- Fold the wet ingredients into the dry ingredients until just combined. Gently fold in the blueberries.
- Spoon the batter into the muffin cases, filling each about two-thirds full.
- Bake for 20-25 minutes, or until a toothpick inserted into the centre of a muffin comes out clean. Allow the muffins to cool in the tin for 5 minutes before transferring them to a wire rack to cool completely..

Carrot Cake Muffins

🕐 **35 minutes**

These delicious carrot muffins are packed with warm spices, grated carrots, and juicy raisins or sultanas. Perfect for breakfast or a snack, they're made with simple ingredients like flour, sugar, eggs, and oil, and are easy to whip up in no time.

Ingredients

200g plain flour
150g granulated sugar
1/2 tsp baking powder
1/2 tsp bicarbonate of soda
1/2 tsp salt
1 tsp ground cinnamon
1/4 tsp ground nutmeg
2 large eggs
120ml vegetable oil
1 tsp vanilla extract
200g grated carrots
100g raisins or sultanas

Method

- Preheat your oven to 180°C (160°C fan/gas mark 4) and line a 12-cup muffin tin with paper cases.
- In a large mixing bowl, whisk together the plain flour, granulated sugar, baking powder, bicarbonate of soda, salt, ground cinnamon, and ground nutmeg.
- In a separate bowl, whisk together the eggs, vegetable oil, and vanilla extract.
- Fold the wet ingredients into the dry ingredients until just combined. Stir in the grated carrots and raisins or sultanas.
- Spoon the batter into the muffin cases, filling each about two-thirds full.
- Bake for 20-25 minutes, or until a toothpick inserted into the centre of a muffin comes out clean. Allow the muffins to cool in the tin for 5 minutes before transferring them to a wire rack to cool completely.

Lemon & Poppy Seed Muffins

🕐 **35 minutes**

These lemon poppy seed muffins are bursting with citrusy flavour. Made with fresh lemon zest, juice, and poppy seeds, they're a bright and delicious breakfast or snack option.

Ingredients

300g plain flour
200g granulated sugar
1/2 tsp salt
3 tsp baking powder
240ml milk
120ml vegetable oil
2 large eggs
Zest of 2 lemons
2 tbsp lemon juice
2 tbsp poppy seeds

Method

- Preheat your oven to 200°C (180°C fan/gas mark 6) and line a 12-cup muffin tin with paper cases.
- In a large mixing bowl, whisk together the plain flour, granulated sugar, salt, and baking powder.
- In a separate bowl, whisk together the milk, vegetable oil, eggs, lemon zest, and lemon juice.
- Fold the wet ingredients into the dry ingredients until just combined. Gently fold in the poppy seeds.
- Spoon the batter into the muffin cases, filling each about two-thirds full.
- Bake for 20-25 minutes, or until a toothpick inserted into the centre of a muffin comes out clean. Allow the muffins to cool in the tin for 5 minutes before transferring them to a wire rack to cool completely.

Cinnamon & Apple Crumble Muffins

🕐 **35 minutes**

Apple crumble muffins are a delightful twist on classic muffins. Packed with chunks of tender apple and topped with a crispy oat crumble, these muffins are moist, fluffy, and full of warm, comforting flavors. Perfect for a cozy breakfast or a comforting afternoon snack.

Ingredients

For the muffins:
250g plain flour
150g granulated sugar
1/2 tsp salt
2 tsp baking powder
1 tsp ground cinnamon
120ml milk
120ml vegetable oil
2 large eggs
1 tsp vanilla extract
2 medium apples, peeled, cored, and diced

For the crumble topping:
50g granulated sugar
50g plain flour
1/2 tsp ground cinnamon
45g unsalted butter, softened

Method

- Preheat your oven to 200°C (180°C fan/gas mark 6) and line a 12-cup muffin tin with paper cases.
- In a large mixing bowl, whisk together the plain flour, granulated sugar, salt, baking powder, and ground cinnamon.
- In a separate bowl, whisk together the milk, vegetable oil, eggs, and vanilla extract.
- Fold the wet ingredients into the dry ingredients until just combined. Gently fold in the diced apples.
- Spoon the batter into the muffin cases, filling each about two-thirds full.
- For the crumble topping:
- In a small mixing bowl, combine the granulated sugar, plain flour, ground cinnamon, and softened butter. Use your fingers or a fork to mix until a crumbly texture is achieved.
- Sprinkle the crumble topping evenly over the muffin batter.
- Bake for 20-25 minutes, or until a toothpick inserted into the centre of a muffin comes out clean. Allow the muffins to cool in the tin for 5 minutes before transferring them to a wire rack to cool completely.

Double Chocolate Muffins

🕐 **30 minutes**

Indulge your chocolate cravings with these rich and decadent chocolate chip muffins. Made with cocoa powder, chocolate chips, and simple ingredients like flour, sugar, milk, and oil, these muffins are moist, fluffy, and perfect for satisfying your sweet tooth any time of day.

Ingredients

250g plain flour
175g granulated sugar
50g unsweetened cocoa powder
1/2 tsp salt
2 tsp baking powder
240ml milk
120ml vegetable oil
2 large eggs
1 tsp vanilla extract
200g chocolate chips

Method

- Preheat your oven to 200°C (180°C fan/gas mark 6) and line a 12-cup muffin tin with paper cases.
- In a large mixing bowl, whisk together the plain flour, granulated sugar, cocoa powder, salt, and baking powder.
- In a separate bowl, whisk together the milk, vegetable oil, eggs, and vanilla extract.
- Fold the wet ingredients into the dry ingredients until just combined. Gently fold in the chocolate chips.
- Spoon the batter into the muffin cases, filling each about two-thirds full.
- Bake for 20-25 minutes, or until a toothpick inserted into the centre of a muffin comes out clean. Allow the muffins to cool in the tin for 5 minutes before transferring them to a wire rack to cool completely.

Raspberry & White Chocolate Muffins

🕐 **35 minutes**

Delightful raspberry white chocolate muffins are made with a soft and fluffy batter filled with juicy raspberries and white chocolate chips. Perfect for breakfast, brunch, or as an indulgent treat.

Ingredients

300g plain flour
150g granulated sugar
1/2 tsp salt
3 tsp baking powder
240ml milk
120ml vegetable oil
2 large eggs
1 tsp vanilla extract
150g fresh or frozen raspberries
150g white chocolate chips

Method

- Preheat your oven to 200°C (180°C fan/gas mark 6) and line a 12-cup muffin tin with paper cases.
- In a large mixing bowl, whisk together the plain flour, granulated sugar, salt, and baking powder.
- In a separate bowl, whisk together the milk, vegetable oil, eggs, and vanilla extract.
- Fold the wet ingredients into the dry ingredients until just combined. Gently fold in the raspberries and white chocolate chips.
- Spoon the batter into the muffin cases, filling each about two-thirds full.
- Bake for 20-25 minutes, or until a toothpick inserted into the centre of a muffin comes out clean. Allow the muffins to cool in the tin for 5 minutes before transferring them to a wire rack to cool completely.

Spinach and Feta Savoury Muffins

🕐 **35 minutes**

These savoury muffins are loaded with healthy spinach and tangy feta cheese. Perfect for breakfast or a midday snack, they are easy to make and full of flavour.

Ingredients

250g plain flour
2 tsp baking powder
1/2 tsp salt
1/4 tsp ground black pepper
200g chopped fresh spinach
100g crumbled feta cheese
240ml milk Write the rest
120ml vegetable oil
2 large eggs

Method

- Preheat your oven to 200°C (180°C fan/gas mark 6) and line a 12-cup muffin tin with paper cases.
- In a large mixing bowl, whisk together the plain flour, baking powder, salt, and ground black pepper.
- Stir in the chopped spinach and crumbled feta cheese, ensuring they are evenly distributed throughout the flour mixture.
- In a separate bowl, whisk together the milk, vegetable oil, and eggs.
- Fold the wet ingredients into the dry ingredients until just combined. Be careful not to overmix.
- Spoon the batter into the muffin cases, filling each about two-thirds full.
- Bake for 20-25 minutes, or until a toothpick inserted into the centre of a muffin comes out clean. Allow the muffins to cool in the tin for 5 minutes before transferring them to a wire rack to cool slightly. These muffins are best enjoyed warm.

Brownie Bonanza
Quick Fixes for Chocolate Cravings

We are exploring a variety of brownie recipes that will satisfy even the most insatiable chocolate cravings. From classic fudgy brownies to exciting twists on this beloved treat, we've got you covered. Let's dive in and discover the delicious world of brownies!

Classic Fudgy Brownies

🕐 **35 minutes**

These rich and indulgent chocolate brownies are made with chopped dark chocolate and cubed butter, giving them a fudgy texture. With just the right amount of sweetness, they're perfect for satisfying your chocolate cravings.

Ingredients

200g dark chocolate, chopped
200g unsalted butter, cubed
300g granulated sugar
3 large eggs
1 tsp vanilla extract
125g plain flour
30g unsweetened cocoa powder
1/2 tsp salt

Method

- Preheat your oven to 180°C (160°C fan/gas mark 4) and line a 20cm square baking tin with baking paper.
- In a heatproof bowl, melt the chopped dark chocolate and cubed butter together over a pan of simmering water, ensuring the bowl doesn't touch the water. Stir until smooth and then remove from heat.
- In a separate bowl, whisk together the granulated sugar, eggs, and vanilla extract until well combined. Pour the melted chocolate mixture into the sugar mixture and stir until combined.
- Sift in the plain flour, cocoa powder, and salt. Gently fold the dry ingredients into the wet ingredients until just combined.
- Pour the brownie batter into the prepared baking tin and smooth the surface with a spatula.
- Bake for 25-30 minutes, or until a toothpick inserted into the centre comes out with a few moist crumbs. Cool the brownies in the tin before cutting into squares.

Blondies

🕐 **35 minutes**

These melt-in-your-mouth blondies are perfect for a sweet treat. With melted butter, light brown sugar, eggs, vanilla extract, flour, baking powder, salt, and white chocolate chips, they're easy to make and even easier to enjoy.

Ingredients

225g unsalted butter, melted
300g light brown sugar
2 large eggs
1 tbsp vanilla extract
250g plain flour
1/2 tsp baking powder
1/2 tsp salt
150g white chocolate chips

Method

- Preheat your oven to 180°C (160°C fan/gas mark 4) and line a 20cm square baking tin with baking paper.
- In a large bowl, mix the melted butter and light brown sugar together until smooth.
- Add the eggs and vanilla extract, mixing well until combined.
- Sift in the plain flour, baking powder, and salt. Gently fold the dry ingredients into the wet ingredients until just combined.
- Stir in the white chocolate chips.
- Pour the blondie batter into the prepared baking tin and smooth the surface with a spatula.
- Bake for 25-30 minutes, or until a toothpick inserted into the centre comes out clean or with a few moist crumbs. Cool the blondies in the tin before cutting them into squares.

Raspberry Swirl Brownies

🕐 **35 minutes**

Indulge in these decadent Raspberry Swirl Brownies, a rich and fudgy chocolate dessert with a swirl of tart raspberry puree. Easy to make with just a few simple ingredients, these brownies are perfect for satisfying your sweet cravings.

Ingredients

For the brownie batter:
200g dark chocolate, chopped
200g unsalted butter, cubed
300g granulated sugar
3 large eggs
1 tsp vanilla extract
125g plain flour
30g unsweetened cocoa powder
1/2 tsp salt

For the raspberry swirl:
150g raspberries, fresh or frozen (thawed if frozen)
50g granulated sugar
1 tbsp cornflour

Method

- Preheat your oven to 180°C (160°C fan/gas mark 4) and line a 20cm square baking tin with baking paper.
- In a heatproof bowl, melt the chopped dark chocolate and cubed butter together over a pan of simmering water, ensuring the bowl doesn't touch the water. Stir until smooth and then remove from heat.
- In a separate bowl, whisk together the granulated sugar, eggs, and vanilla extract until well combined. Pour the melted chocolate mixture into the sugar mixture and stir until combined.
- Sift in the plain flour, cocoa powder, and salt. Gently fold the dry ingredients into the wet ingredients until just combined.
- To make the raspberry swirl, in a blender or food processor, purée the raspberries, sugar, and cornflour until smooth. Pass the mixture through a fine-mesh sieve to remove the seeds.
- Pour the brownie batter into the prepared baking tin and smooth the surface with a spatula. Spoon dollops of the raspberry purée on top of the brownie batter. Use a skewer or knife to swirl the raspberry purée into the brownie batter, creating a marbled effect.
- Bake for 25-30 minutes, or until a toothpick inserted into the centre comes out with a few moist crumbs. Cool the brownies in the tin before cutting them into squares.

Peanut Butter Brownies

🕐 **35 minutes**

Peanut Butter Brownies are the perfect indulgent treat for any peanut butter lover. Rich and fudgy brownies are swirled with creamy peanut butter for a decadent dessert that is easy to make and sure to impress.

Ingredients

For the brownie batter:
200g dark chocolate, chopped
200g unsalted butter, cubed
300g granulated sugar
3 large eggs
1 tsp vanilla extract
125g plain flour
30g unsweetened cocoa powder
1/2 tsp salt

For the peanut butter swirl:
125g smooth peanut butter
50g granulated sugar
1 large egg
1/2 tsp vanilla extract

Method

- Preheat your oven to 180°C (160°C fan/gas mark 4) and line a 20cm square baking tin with baking paper.
- In a heatproof bowl, melt the chopped dark chocolate and cubed butter together over a pan of simmering water, ensuring the bowl doesn't touch the water. Stir until smooth and then remove from heat.
- In a separate bowl, whisk together the granulated sugar, eggs, and vanilla extract until well combined. Pour the melted chocolate mixture into the sugar mixture and stir until combined.
- Sift in the plain flour, cocoa powder, and salt. Gently fold the dry ingredients into the wet ingredients until just combined.
- To make the peanut butter swirl, in a separate bowl, mix together the peanut butter, sugar, egg, and vanilla extract until smooth.
- Pour the brownie batter into the prepared baking tin and smooth the surface with a spatula. Spoon dollops of the peanut butter mixture on top of the brownie batter. Use a skewer or knife to swirl the peanut butter mixture into the brownie batter, creating a marbled effect.
- Bake for 25-30 minutes, or until a toothpick inserted into the centre comes out with a few moist crumbs. Cool the brownies in the tin before cutting them into squares.

Salted Caramel Brownies

🕐 **35 minutes**

Indulge in the perfect balance of sweet and salty with these decadent salted caramel brownies. Fudgy and rich, these brownies are swirled with caramel and sprinkled with sea salt, making them a heavenly dessert for any occasion.

Ingredients

For the brownie batter:
200g dark chocolate, chopped
200g unsalted butter, cubed
300g granulated sugar
3 large eggs
1 tsp vanilla extract
125g plain flour
30g unsweetened cocoa powder
1/2 tsp salt

For the salted caramel:
200g granulated sugar
90g unsalted butter, cubed
120ml double cream
1 tsp sea salt flakes

Method

- Preheat your oven to 180°C (160°C fan/gas mark 4) and line a 20cm square baking tin with baking paper.
- Make a delicious salted caramel brownie by melting dark chocolate and butter together.
- Whisk sugar, eggs, and vanilla extract in a separate bowl.
- Add melted chocolate to the mixture and fold in plain flour, cocoa powder, and salt.
- Heat sugar in a saucepan until it turns amber in colour.
- Add butter, then double cream and sea salt flakes.
- Pour half the brownie mixture into a lined baking tin, add half the caramel, pour the remaining batter on top and add remaining caramel.
- Bake for 25-30 mins and cool before serving.

Espresso Brownies

🕐 **35 minutes**

These espresso brownies are the perfect combination of rich, chocolatey flavour and a bold espresso kick. With a fudgy texture and a deep, complex flavour, they are sure to satisfy any coffee lover's cravings.

Ingredients

For the Brownies:
225g (2 sticks) of unsalted butter
225g semi-sweet chocolate, chopped
300g granulated sugar
4 large eggs, at room temperature
1 tsp pure vanilla extract
60ml espresso or strong brewed coffee cooled
140g all-purpose flour
50g unsweetened cocoa powder
1/4 tsp salt
2 tsp instant espresso powder

For the Espresso Glaze:
125g powdered sugar
15g unsalted butter, melted

Method

- Line a 9x13-inch baking pan with parchment paper.
- Melt butter and chocolate in a microwave-safe bowl, set aside to cool.
- In a separate bowl, whisk sugar, eggs, vanilla extract, and espresso.
- Gradually add chocolate mixture and mix well.
- Combine flour, cocoa powder, salt, and instant espresso powder in another bowl. Add dry ingredients to wet mixture and mix until combined.
- Pour into pan and bake for 30-35 mins.
- For the espresso glaze, whisk powdered sugar, melted butter, and espresso together until smooth.
- Add more espresso for desired consistency.
- Cool brownies before drizzling glaze on top.

Black Bean Brownies

🕐 **35 minutes**

Black bean brownies are a gluten-free and healthier alternative to traditional brownies. Made with black beans, cocoa powder, eggs, and maple syrup, they're rich and fudgy. Serve them as a guilt-free treat or snack.

Ingredients

400g tin of black beans, drained and rinsed
2 large eggs
60g unsweetened cocoa powder
150g granulated sugar
60ml vegetable oil
1 tbsp vanilla extract
1/4 tsp salt
1/2 tsp baking powder
100g dark chocolate chips

Method

- Preheat your oven to 180°C (160°C fan/gas mark 4) and line a 20cm square baking tin with baking paper.
- In a food processor or blender, combine the black beans, eggs, cocoa powder, sugar, vegetable oil, vanilla extract, salt, and baking powder. Process until smooth and well combined.
- Stir in the dark chocolate chips by hand.
- Pour the brownie batter into the prepared baking tin and smooth the surface with a spatula.
- Bake for 25-30 minutes, or until a toothpick inserted into the centre comes out clean or with a few moist crumbs. Cool the brownies in the tin before cutting them into squares.

Cheesecake Brownies

🕐 **35 minutes**

Enjoy rich chocolate brownies with a tangy cheesecake swirl in this recipe. The fudgy base complements the creamy topping for a balanced sweetness and tartness. Perfect for dessert lovers torn between chocolate and cheesecake.

Ingredients

For the brownie batter:

200g dark chocolate, chopped

200g unsalted butter, cubed

300g granulated sugar

3 large eggs

1 tsp vanilla extract

125g plain flour

30g unsweetened cocoa powder

1/2 tsp salt

For the cheesecake layer:

225g cream cheese, softened

75g granulated sugar

1 large egg

1/2 tsp vanilla extract

Method

- Preheat your oven to 180°C (160°C fan/gas mark 4) and line a 20cm square baking tin with baking paper.
- In a heatproof bowl, melt the chopped dark chocolate and cubed butter together over a pan of simmering water, ensuring the bowl doesn't touch the water. Stir until smooth and then remove from heat.
- In a separate bowl, whisk together the granulated sugar, eggs, and vanilla extract until well combined. Pour the melted chocolate mixture into the sugar mixture and stir until combined.
- Sift in the plain flour, cocoa powder, and salt. Gently fold the dry ingredients into the wet ingredients until just combined.
- To make the cheesecake layer, in a separate bowl, beat the cream cheese and sugar together until smooth. Add the egg and vanilla extract, and beat until well combined.
- Pour the brownie batter into the prepared baking tin and smooth the surface with a spatula. Spoon dollops of the cheesecake mixture on top of the brownie batter. Use a skewer or knife to swirl the cheesecake mixture into the brownie batter, creating a marbled effect.
- Bake for 25-30 minutes, or until a toothpick inserted into the centre comes out with a few moist crumbs. Cool the brownies in the tin before cutting into squares.

Instant Indulgence
No-Bake Desserts for Every Occasion

Welcome to the world of no-bake desserts, where you can indulge in delightful sweets without ever switching on the oven! This chapter is dedicated to those moments when time is tight, or you simply prefer a fuss-free approach to satisfying your cravings.

From chilled confections to simple fridge cakes, we've curated a selection of mouth-watering treats that cater to all tastes and occasions. So, whether you're planning a cosy gathering with friends, a family celebration, or just looking for an easy dessert to enjoy at home, you're sure to find the perfect recipe in this chapter.

No-Bake Chocolate Truffles

🕐 25 minutes

Decadent and indulgent, these chocolate truffles are a bite-sized treat that are perfect for satisfying your sweet tooth. Made with rich chocolate ganache and rolled in cocoa powder or chopped nuts.

Ingredients

300g dark chocolate, finely chopped

200ml double cream

2 tbsp unsalted butter, at room temperature

1 tsp vanilla extract

5g Cocoa powder, for dusting

Method

- Place the finely chopped dark chocolate in a heatproof bowl.
- In a saucepan, heat the double cream over medium heat until it's steaming but not boiling. Pour the hot cream over the chopped chocolate, ensuring it's completely covered. Let the mixture sit for 2-3 minutes to allow the chocolate to soften.
- Stir the chocolate and cream mixture until smooth and well combined. Add the unsalted butter and vanilla extract, and mix until the butter is fully incorporated and the mixture is glossy.
- Cover the bowl with cling film and refrigerate for at least 2 hours, or until the mixture is firm enough to hold its shape.
- Prepare a baking sheet lined with parchment paper. Using a small spoon or a melon baller, scoop out portions of the chilled chocolate mixture and roll them into balls using your hands. Place the truffles on the prepared baking sheet.
- Once all truffles are formed, place them in the refrigerator for an additional 15-20 minutes to firm up.
- Place cocoa powder in a shallow dish. Roll each truffle in the cocoa powder to coat them evenly. Shake off any excess cocoa powder.
- Store the truffles in an airtight container in the refrigerator until ready to serve. Allow the truffles to sit at room temperature for 10-15 minutes before serving for the best texture.

Raspberry & White Chocolate Cheesecake

🕐 **35 minutes**

Creamy white chocolate cheesecake swirled with a tart raspberry sauce and a crunchy biscuit base. A perfect balance of sweet and tangy flavors, this dessert is a crowd-pleaser.

Ingredients

For the crust:
200g digestive biscuits, crushed
100g unsalted butter, melted

For the filling:
500g cream cheese, softened
100g icing sugar
1 tsp vanilla extract
200ml double cream, whipped
200g white chocolate, melted and cooled
200g fresh raspberries

Method

- In a bowl, combine the crushed digestive biscuits and melted butter. Press the mixture into the bottom of a 20cm springform tin, ensuring it's evenly distributed and compact. Refrigerate for at least 30 minutes to set the crust.
- In a separate large bowl, beat the cream cheese, icing sugar, and vanilla extract together until smooth and creamy.
- In another bowl, whip the double cream until soft peaks form.
- Melt the white chocolate in a heatproof bowl over a pan of simmering water, ensuring the bowl doesn't touch the water. Stir until smooth, then remove from heat and let it cool slightly.
- Gently fold the whipped double cream and melted white chocolate into the cream cheese mixture until well combined.
- Carefully fold in the fresh raspberries, reserving a few for decoration. Make sure to fold gently to avoid crushing the raspberries.
- Pour the cream cheese mixture over the chilled biscuit crust, smoothing the surface with a spatula.
- Refrigerate the cheesecake for at least 4 hours, or preferably overnight, until it is set.
- Once set, carefully remove the cheesecake from the springform tin. Decorate the top of the cheesecake with the reserved raspberries.
- Serve the cheesecake chilled, and store any leftovers in the refrigerator.

Frozen Banana & Peanut Butter Bites

🕐 **15 minutes**

These Frozen Banana and Peanut Butter Bites are a simple and delicious snack.

Ingredients

4 large ripe bananas, peeled and
sliced into 1/2-inch (1.3 cm)
rounds
200g smooth peanut butter
400g dark chocolate, chopped

Method

- Line a baking tray with parchment paper.
- Lay out half of the banana slices on the prepared baking tray.
- Spread a small amount of peanut butter onto each banana slice on the tray, making sure not to use too much, as you don't want it to overflow when the bites are assembled.
- Place another banana slice on top of each peanut butter-covered slice, creating a sandwich with the peanut butter in the middle. Press down gently to ensure the slices stick together.
- Freeze the banana sandwiches on the tray for at least 1 hour, or until they are firm.
- Melt the chopped dark chocolate in a heatproof bowl over a pan of simmering water, ensuring the bowl doesn't touch the water. Stir until smooth and then remove from heat.
- Remove the frozen banana sandwiches from the freezer. Using a fork or a skewer, dip each sandwich into the melted chocolate, making sure to coat all sides evenly.
- Place the chocolate-covered banana bites back onto the parchment-lined tray.
- Coat the banana bites in chocolate, freeze them again for at least 30 minutes, or until the chocolate has set.
- Transfer the frozen banana and peanut butter bites to an airtight container and store them in the freezer until ready to serve. Enjoy these treats straight from the freezer for a refreshing and delicious snack!

Oreo Cookie Balls

🕐 **35 minutes**

These Oreo Cookie Balls are a no-bake dessert made with just three ingredients: crushed Oreos, cream cheese, and melted chocolate. Perfect for parties or a sweet treat at home.

Ingredients

250g Oreo cookies
225g cream cheese, softened
200g white chocolate, chopped
Optional: Crushed Oreo cookies
or sprinkles, for decoration

Method

- Crush Oreo cookies
- Blend with softened cream cheese in a food processor.
- Roll mixture into small balls and freeze for 30 minutes.
- Dip balls in melted white chocolate and decorate if desired.
- Refrigerate until chocolate sets.

Mango and Coconut Panna Cotta

🕐 **25 minutes**

A silky smooth dessert with a tropical twist, this Mango and Coconut Panna Cotta features layers of creamy coconut and sweet mango, perfect for a refreshing treat on a warm day.

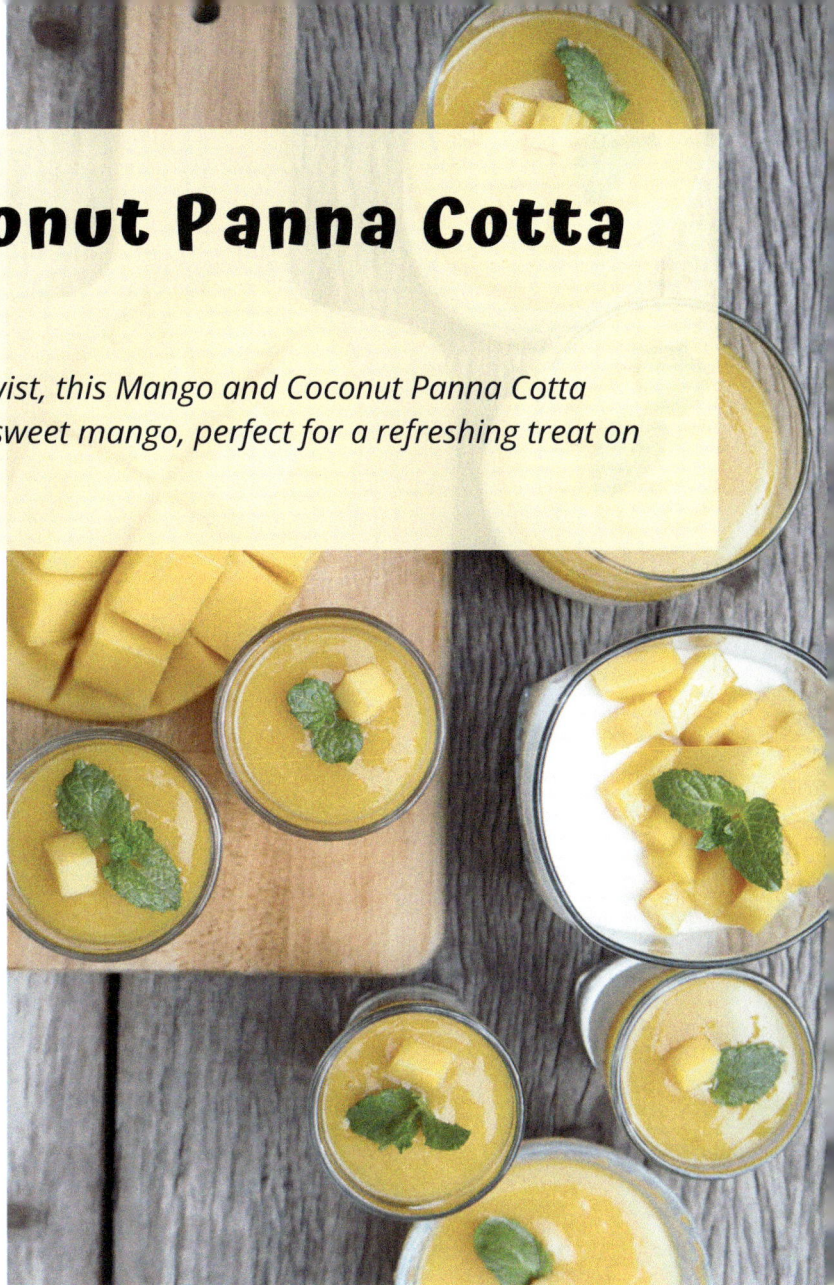

Ingredients

400ml coconut milk
100ml double cream
100g caster sugar
2 tsp powdered gelatine
2 tbsp cold water
1 large ripe mango, peeled and chopped

Method

- In a saucepan, heat the coconut milk, double cream, and caster sugar over low heat, occasionally stirring until the sugar dissolves. Remove from heat.
- In a small bowl, sprinkle the powdered gelatine over the cold water and let it sit for 5 minutes to soften.
- Add the softened gelatine to the warm coconut milk mixture and stir until completely dissolved.
- Divide the mixture evenly among individual serving glasses or ramekins. Refrigerate for at least 4 hours, or until set.
- Before serving, prepare the mango topping. Peel and chop the ripe mango into small pieces.
- Top each panna cotta with the chopped mango.
- Serve the mango and coconut panna cotta chilled and enjoy this refreshing dessert!

No-Bake Chocolate Peanut Butter Bars

🕒 **15 minutes**

Indulge in these rich and decadent peanut butter chocolate bars with a buttery biscuit base. Topped with a smooth layer of sweetened peanut butter and coated in creamy milk chocolate, they're the perfect sweet treat.

Ingredients

200g digestive biscuits, crushed

100g unsalted butter, melted

200g smooth peanut butter

200g milk chocolate, chopped

50g icing sugar

Method

- Line a 20cm square tin with baking paper.
- In a large bowl, mix the crushed digestive biscuits with the melted butter, 150g of peanut butter, and icing sugar until well combined.
- Press the mixture into the prepared tin, ensuring it's evenly distributed and compact.
- Melt the milk chocolate and the remaining 50g of peanut butter in a heatproof bowl over a pan of simmering water, ensuring the bowl doesn't touch the water. Stir until smooth and then remove from heat.
- Pour the chocolate mixture over the biscuit layer, spreading it evenly.
- Refrigerate for at least 2 hours, or until set. Remove from the tin and cut into squares. Store the bars in an airtight container in the refrigerator.

No-Bake Mini Cheesecakes

🕐 **25 minutes**

These No-Bake Mini Cheesecakes are a perfect dessert for hot summer days. With a buttery digestive biscuit crust and creamy cheesecake filling, they're quick and easy to make, and totally delicious.

Ingredients

For the crust:
200g digestive biscuits, crushed
100g unsalted butter, melted

For the filling:
500g cream cheese, softened
100g icing sugar
1 tsp vanilla extract
200ml double cream, whipped

Method

- Line a 12-cup muffin tin with paper liners.
- In a bowl, mix the crushed digestive biscuits and melted butter. Divide the mixture among the muffin cups, pressing it down to create an even layer.
- In a separate large bowl, beat the cream cheese, icing sugar, and vanilla extract together until smooth and creamy.
- In another bowl, whip the double cream until soft peaks form.
- Gently fold the whipped double cream into the cream cheese mixture until well combined.
- Spoon the filling over the biscuit crust in each muffin cup.
- Refrigerate the mini cheesecakes for at least 4 hours, or until set.
- When ready to serve, carefully remove the paper liners from the cheesecakes. Top with your choice of fresh fruit, chocolate shavings, or a drizzle of caramel sauce.

Cake in a Flash
Simple and Scrumptious Single-Layer Cakes

In this chapter, we'll be exploring a delightful array of single-layer cake recipes perfect for when you're short on time but still craving a scrumptious homemade dessert. From fruity delights to classic chocolatey treats, these recipes are not only quick and easy to prepare but also irresistibly tasty. With these delicious single-layer cake recipes, you'll be well-equipped to whip up a mouth-watering dessert at a moment's notice. From casual gatherings to special occasions, these cakes are sure to impress your friends and family. So, without further ado, let's dive into these fantastic recipes and start baking!

Easy Vanilla Sponge Cake

🕐 **35 minutes**

This easy vanilla sponge cake is light, fluffy, and perfect for any occasion. Made with simple ingredients and baked to golden perfection, it's a classic treat that everyone will love.

Ingredients

200g unsalted butter, softened, plus extra for greasing

200g caster sugar

4 large eggs

200g self-raising flour

1 tsp baking powder

2 tsp vanilla extract

Optional: Icing sugar, for dusting

Method

- Preheat your oven to 180°C (350°F). Grease a 20cm round cake tin with butter and line the bottom with baking paper.
- In a large mixing bowl, cream the softened butter and caster sugar together until light and fluffy, using an electric mixer or a wooden spoon.
- Add the eggs one at a time, mixing well after each addition. If the mixture looks like it's curdling, add a tablespoon of flour to help it come together.
- Sift the self-raising flour and baking powder into the mixing bowl. Add the vanilla extract and gently fold the dry ingredients into the wet mixture, using a spatula or a large metal spoon, until just combined. Be careful not to overmix, as this will result in a dense cake.
- Pour the cake batter into the prepared tin and level the top with a spatula or the back of a spoon.
- Bake the cake in the preheated oven for 25-30 minutes, or until a skewer inserted into the centre comes out clean. If the cake starts to brown too quickly, cover it with a piece of aluminium foil.
- Remove the cake from the oven and let it cool in the tin for about 10 minutes. Then, carefully turn it out onto a wire rack to cool completely.
- Optional: Once the cake has cooled, you can dust it with icing sugar for a simple yet elegant finish.

One-Bowl Chocolate Cake

🕐 **35 minutes**

Indulge in the rich and chocolatey goodness of this one-bowl cake, made with simple ingredients and minimal clean-up.
Perfect for satisfying your chocolate cravings in no time!

Ingredients

200g all-purpose flour

200g granulated sugar

75g unsweetened cocoa powder

1 1/2 tsp baking powder

1 1/2 tsp baking soda

1/2 tsp salt

2 large eggs

240ml whole milk

120ml vegetable oil

2 tsp vanilla extract

240ml boiling water

Method

- Preheat oven to 175°C (350°F).
- Grease and line a 20cm round cake tin.
- In a bowl, whisk flour, sugar, cocoa, baking powder, baking soda, and salt.
- Add eggs, milk, oil, and vanilla. Mix until smooth.
- Pour boiling water into the batter and stir until combined.
- Pour batter into the tin and bake for 30-35 mins.
- Cool in the tin for 10 mins, then transfer to a wire rack to cool completely.
- Frost with icing or dust with sugar/cocoa powder.
- Serve with ice cream or whipped cream. Enjoy!

Lemon Drizzle Cake

🕐 **60 minutes**

A classic British cake, lemon drizzle cake is a moist and tangy treat, topped with a zesty lemon syrup. Perfect for afternoon tea or a sweet snack.

Ingredients

For the cake:
225g unsalted butter, softened, plus extra for greasing
225g caster sugar
4 large eggs
225g self-raising flour
Finely grated zest of 2 lemons

For the drizzle:
Juice of 2 lemons
120g icing sugar

Method

- Preheat oven to 180°C (350°F).
- Grease and line a 20cm x 12cm loaf tin.
- Cream butter and sugar until fluffy.
- Add eggs one at a time, then sift in flour and lemon zest.
- Fold until just combined.
- Pour batter into tin and bake for 45-50 minutes.
- Mix lemon juice and icing sugar for the drizzle.
- When the cake is done, poke holes in it and pour the drizzle over the top.
- Cool in the tin, then remove and transfer to a plate.

Spiced Carrot Cake

🕐 **60 minutes**

This spiced carrot cake is a deliciously moist and flavorful cake, packed with grated carrots, warm spices, and a creamy cream cheese frosting. Perfect for any occasion.

Ingredients

200g all-purpose flour
200g granulated sugar
1 1/2 tsp baking powder
1 1/2 tsp baking soda
1/2 tsp salt
2 tsp ground cinnamon
1/2 tsp ground nutmeg
1/2 tsp ground ginger
3 large eggs
180ml vegetable oil
1 tsp vanilla extract
300g grated carrots
100g chopped walnuts or pecans (optional)

For the cream cheese frosting:
100g unsalted butter, softened
200g cream cheese, softened
400g icing sugar
1 tsp vanilla extract

Method

- Preheat your oven to 180°C (350°F). Grease a 20cm x 12cm loaf tin with butter and line the bottom and sides with baking paper.
- In a large mixing bowl, cream the softened butter and caster sugar together until light and fluffy, using an electric mixer or a wooden spoon.
- Add the eggs one at a time, mixing well after each addition. If the mixture looks like it's curdling, add a tablespoon of flour to help it come together.
- Sift the self-raising flour into the mixing bowl. Add the finely grated lemon zest and gently fold the dry ingredients into the wet mixture, using a spatula or a large metal spoon, until just combined. Be careful not to overmix, as this will result in a dense cake.
- Pour the cake batter into the prepared tin and level the top with a spatula or the back of a spoon.
- Bake the cake in the preheated oven for 45-50 minutes, or until a skewer inserted into the centre comes out clean.

Method

- While the cake is baking, prepare the drizzle. In a small bowl, mix the lemon juice
- and icing sugar until well combined and smooth.
- When the cake is done, remove it from the oven and leave it to cool in the tin for about 10 minutes. Use a skewer to poke holes all over the top of the warm cake, going about halfway through.
- Slowly pour the lemon drizzle mixture over the top of the cake, allowing it to soak in.
- Leave the cake to cool completely in the tin.
- Once the cake has cooled, carefully remove it from the tin, and transfer it to a serving plate.

Blueberry & Lemon Yogurt Cake

🕐 **60 Minutes**

This Blueberry & Lemon Yogurt Cake is a deliciously moist and flavourful dessert. Bursting with juicy blueberries and tangy lemon, this cake is perfect for any occasion.

Ingredients

225g all-purpose flour
2 tsp baking powder
1/2 tsp salt
225g granulated sugar
Zest of 2 lemons
120ml plain yoghurt (full fat or low fat)
3 large eggs
1/2 tsp vanilla extract
120ml vegetable oil
250g fresh blueberries

For the lemon glaze (optional):
Juice of 1 lemon
100g icing sugar

Method

- Preheat your oven to 180°C (350°F). Grease a 20cm round cake tin with butter or cooking spray, and line the bottom with baking paper.
- In a medium-sized mixing bowl, whisk together the all-purpose flour, baking powder, and salt. Set aside.
- In a large mixing bowl, combine the granulated sugar and lemon zest. Use your fingers to rub the zest into the sugar, releasing the lemon oil and creating a fragrant, lemon-infused sugar.
- Add the yogurt, eggs, and vanilla extract to the lemon sugar. Whisk until smooth and well combined.
- Gradually add the dry ingredients to the wet ingredients, stirring until just combined.
- Slowly pour the vegetable oil into the batter, folding it in gently until fully incorporated.
- Gently fold in about two-thirds of the blueberries, being careful not to overmix the batter.

Method

- Pour the cake batter into the prepared tin, leveling the top with a spatula or the back of a spoon. Scatter the remaining blueberries over the top of the batter.
- Bake the cake in the preheated oven for 45-50 minutes, or until a skewer inserted into the center comes out clean.
- Remove the cake from the oven and let it cool in the tin for about 15 minutes. Then, carefully turn it out onto a wire rack to cool completely.
- While the cake cools, you can prepare the optional lemon glaze. In a small bowl, mix the lemon juice and icing sugar until smooth and well combined.
- Once the cake has cooled, drizzle the lemon glaze over the top, allowing it to run down the sides. Alternatively, you can dust the cake with icing sugar for a simpler finish.
- Serve your blueberry and lemon yogurt cake as a delightful dessert or an afternoon treat with a cup of tea. Enjoy!

Sticky Toffee Pudding Cake

🕐 **50 minutes**

Indulge in a decadent and moist Sticky Toffee Pudding Cake, with a rich caramel flavour and sweet toffee sauce. Perfect for satisfying your sweet tooth cravings.

Ingredients

200g pitted dates, chopped
240ml boiling water
1 tsp bicarbonate of soda
75g unsalted butter, softened
175g light brown sugar
2 large eggs
175g all-purpose flour
1 tsp baking powder
1/2 tsp salt

For the toffee sauce:
100g unsalted butter
150g light brown sugar
150ml double cream
1/2 tsp vanilla extract

Method

- Preheat oven to 180°C (350°F).
- Grease a 20cm square cake tin and line with baking paper.
- Pour boiling water over chopped dates and bicarbonate of soda in a small bowl, set aside.
- Cream butter and light brown sugar in a large mixing bowl.
- Add eggs one at a time, mixing well. In a separate bowl, whisk flour, baking powder, and salt.
- Add to butter mixture alternately with date mixture.
- Pour batter into prepared tin and level with a spatula. Bake for 35-40 minutes.
- Make toffee sauce by melting butter in a saucepan.
- Add sugar and stir until combined.
- Add double cream and vanilla.
- Let cake cool in the tin for 10 minutes before serving with the toffee sauce.

Method

- Use a skewer to poke several holes all over the top of the warm cake, going about halfway through.
- Slowly pour the toffee sauce over the top of the cake, allowing it to soak in. Reserve some of the sauce to drizzle over each slice of cake when serving.
- Leave the cake to cool for a few minutes before slicing it and serving it warm with a drizzle of toffee sauce on top. Enjoy!

Zesty Orange Polenta Cake

🕐 **50 minutes**

This gluten-free Zesty Orange Polenta Cake is made with finely ground polenta, giving it a delicate and moist texture, and is infused with fresh orange zest for a bright and tangy flavour.

Ingredients

200g unsalted butter, softened
200g caster sugar
4 large eggs
200g ground almonds
150g fine polenta
2 tsp baking powder
Zest of 2 oranges
Juice of 1 orange
Icing sugar, for dusting

Method

- Preheat oven to 160°C (320°F).
- Grease a 20cm round cake tin with butter or cooking spray, and line the bottom with baking paper.
- In a bowl, cream softened butter and caster sugar until fluffy, add eggs one at a time, mix well. In a separate bowl, mix ground almonds, fine polenta, and baking powder.
- Gradually mix dry ingredients into wet ingredients. Stir in orange zest and juice. Pour batter into tin and level top with spatula.
- Bake for 40-45 minutes or until a skewer comes out clean.
- Cool for 10 minutes in tin, then turn out onto wire rack to cool completely. Optionally, dust with icing sugar.
- Serve as is or with whipped cream or vanilla ice cream. Enjoy!

Flourless Chocolate Cake

🕐 **40 minutes**

This decadent Flourless Chocolate Cake is a rich and fudgy dessert made with just a few simple ingredients, including dark chocolate, eggs, and butter. Perfect for chocolate lovers and gluten-free diets.

Ingredients

200g dark chocolate (70% cocoa solids), chopped
200g unsalted butter, cut into cubes
5 large eggs, separated
200g caster sugar
1 tsp vanilla extract
1/4 tsp salt

Method

- Preheat oven to 180°C (350°F).
- Grease and line a 20cm round cake tin.
- Melt the dark chocolate and butter in a heatproof bowl set over a pan of simmering water.
- Set aside to cool.
- Whisk egg yolks, sugar, vanilla extract, and salt until pale and fluffy.
- In a separate bowl, whisk egg whites until stiff peaks form.
- Combine cooled chocolate mixture with the egg yolk mixture.
- Gently fold in whisked egg whites.
- Pour batter into the prepared tin and level the top.
- Bake for 30-35 minutes.
- Cool in the tin for 10 minutes then turn onto a wire rack to cool completely.

Cupcake Craze

Quick Tips for Creative Cupcake Decorating

Welcome to the wonderful world of cupcakes! From classic vanilla and chocolate to fun and creative flavours like red velvet and matcha, cupcakes are a favourite treat for all ages. But why settle for plain and boring cupcakes when you can take your decorating skills to the next level?

In this chapter, we'll share some quick tips and tricks for creative cupcake decorating that will impress your friends and family. From simple but effective frosting techniques to fun and festive toppings, you'll learn how to turn your cupcakes into edible works of art.

But before we dive into the decorating, let's start with some delicious cupcake recipes to get you started.
Here are 7 mouth-watering cupcake recipes for you to try:

Classic Vanilla Cupcakes

🕐 **25 minutes**

Moist and fluffy vanilla cupcakes topped with a creamy buttercream frosting. These classic cupcakes are simple to make and perfect for any occasion, from birthdays to afternoon tea.

Ingredients

150g all-purpose flour
1 tsp baking powder
1/4 tsp salt
115g unsalted butter, softened
150g granulated sugar
2 large eggs
2 tsp vanilla extract
120ml milk

Method

- Preheat your oven to 180°C (350°F). Line a 12-cup muffin tin with paper cupcake liners.
- In a medium bowl, whisk together the all-purpose flour, baking powder, and salt.
- In a large mixing bowl, cream the softened butter and granulated sugar together until light and fluffy, using an electric mixer or a wooden spoon.
- Add the eggs one at a time, mixing well after each addition.
- Stir in the vanilla extract until evenly distributed.
- Gradually add the dry ingredients to the wet ingredients, alternating with the milk, mixing until just combined.
- Pour the cupcake batter into the lined muffin tin, filling each cupcake liner about two-thirds full.
- Bake the cupcakes in the preheated oven for 18-20 minutes, or until a skewer inserted into the center comes out clean.
- Remove the cupcakes from the oven and let them cool in the muffin tin for a few minutes. Then, transfer them to a wire rack to cool completely.
- Once the cupcakes are cool, you can frost and decorate them as desired. Enjoy your classic vanilla cupcakes!

Double Chocolate Cupcakes

🕐 **25 minutes**

Indulge in rich and decadent double chocolate cupcakes. Moist and chocolatey with a chocolate ganache frosting, these cupcakes are perfect for satisfying your sweet tooth.

Ingredients

150g all-purpose flour

50g cocoa powder

1 tsp baking powder

1/2 tsp baking soda

1/4 tsp salt

115g unsalted butter, softened

150g granulated sugar

2 large eggs

1 tsp vanilla extract

120ml milk

100g dark chocolate chips

Method

- Preheat oven to 180°C (350°F).
- Line a muffin tin with paper liners.
- Whisk flour, cocoa powder, baking powder, baking soda, and salt in a medium bowl.
- Cream butter and sugar in a large mixing bowl.
- Add eggs and vanilla extract, mixing well after each addition.
- Gradually add dry ingredients to wet mixture, alternating with milk.
- Fold in dark chocolate chips.
- Pour batter into muffin tin, filling each liner 2/3 full. Bake for 18-20 minutes or until a skewer inserted into the center comes out clean.
- Cool cupcakes in the muffin tin for a few minutes, then transfer to a wire rack to cool completely. Frost and decorate as desired.

Red Velvet Cupcakes

🕐 **25 minutes**

Indulge in the rich, velvety goodness of classic Red Velvet cupcakes. Topped with a fluffy cream cheese frosting, these cupcakes are the perfect dessert for any occasion.

Ingredients

150g all-purpose flour

1 tbsp cocoa powder

1/2 tsp baking soda

1/4 tsp salt

115g unsalted butter, softened

150g granulated sugar

2 large eggs

1 tsp vanilla extract

1 tbsp red food coloring

120ml buttermilk

1/2 tsp white vinegar

1/2 tsp baking powder

Method

- Preheat your oven to 180°C (350°F). Line a 12-cup muffin tin with paper cupcake liners.
- In a medium bowl, whisk together the all-purpose flour, cocoa powder, baking soda, and salt.
- In a large mixing bowl, cream the softened butter and granulated sugar together until light and fluffy, using an electric mixer or a wooden spoon.
- Add the eggs one at a time, mixing well after each addition.
- Stir in the vanilla extract and red food coloring until evenly distributed.
- Gradually add the dry ingredients to the wet ingredients, alternating with the buttermilk, mixing until just combined.
- In a small bowl, mix together the white vinegar and baking powder until foamy. Fold it into the cupcake batter.
- Pour the cupcake batter into the lined muffin tin, filling each cupcake liner about two-thirds full.

Method

- Bake the cupcakes in the preheated oven for 18-20 minutes, or until a skewer inserted into the center comes out clean.
- Remove the cupcakes from the oven and let them cool in the muffin tin for a few minutes. Then, transfer them to a wire rack to cool completely.
- Once the cupcakes are cool, you can frost and decorate them as desired. Enjoy your delicious red velvet cupcakes!

Lemon and Blueberry Cupcakes

🕐 **25 minutes**

These lemon blueberry cupcakes are a delightful treat! Made with fresh blueberries and lemon zest, they are light, fluffy, and perfect for any occasion.

Ingredients

150g all-purpose flour
1 tsp baking powder
1/4 tsp salt
115g unsalted butter, softened
150g granulated sugar
2 large eggs
1 tsp vanilla extract
1 lemon, zest and juice
120ml milk
100g fresh blueberries

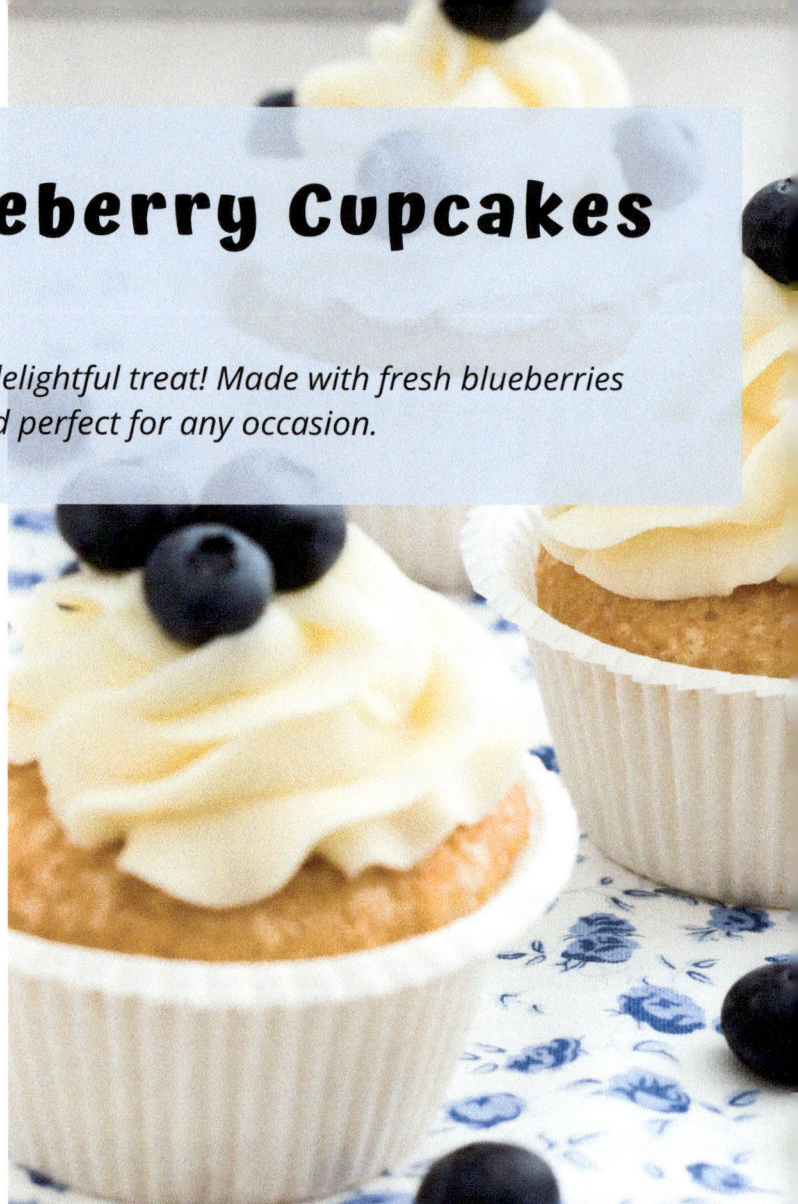

Method

- Preheat oven to 180°C (350°F) and line a 12-cup muffin tin with paper liners.
- Whisk together flour, baking powder, and salt in a medium bowl.
- In a large mixing bowl, cream softened butter and granulated sugar until light and fluffy.
- Add eggs one at a time, mixing well. Stir in vanilla extract, lemon zest and juice. Gradually add dry ingredients and milk, mixing until just combined.
- Fold in fresh blueberries.
- Pour batter into lined muffin tin, filling each cupcake liner about two-thirds full.
- Bake for 18-20 minutes or until a skewer comes out clean.
- Let cool and decorate as desired.
- Enjoy lemon blueberry cupcakes!

Matcha Green Tea Cupcakes

🕐 **25 minutes**

These matcha cupcakes are a unique twist on the classic vanilla cupcake, with a vibrant green color and a hint of earthy matcha flavor in the cake and frosting.

Ingredients

150g all-purpose flour

1 tsp baking powder

1/4 tsp salt

115g unsalted butter, softened

150g granulated sugar

2 large eggs

2 tbsp matcha green tea powder

1 tsp vanilla extract

120ml milk

Method

- Preheat oven to 180°C (350°F) and line 12-cup muffin tin with liners.
- In a medium bowl, whisk together flour, baking powder, and salt.
- In a large mixing bowl, cream softened butter and granulated sugar until light and fluffy. Add eggs one at a time, mixing well.
- Stir in matcha green tea powder and vanilla extract until evenly distributed. Gradually add dry ingredients to wet ingredients, alternating with milk, mixing until just combined.
- Pour batter into lined muffin tin, filling each liner about two-thirds full.
- Bake for 18-20 minutes, or until a skewer inserted into the center comes out clean.
- Cool in muffin tin for a few minutes, then transfer to wire rack to cool completely.
- Frost and decorate as desired. Enjoy your delicious matcha green tea cupcakes!

Salted Caramel Cupcakes

🕐 **25 minutes**

Indulge in the sweet and salty goodness of Salted Caramel Cupcakes! Moist vanilla cupcakes with a luscious salted caramel frosting topped with a sprinkle of sea salt for the perfect balance of flavours.

Ingredients

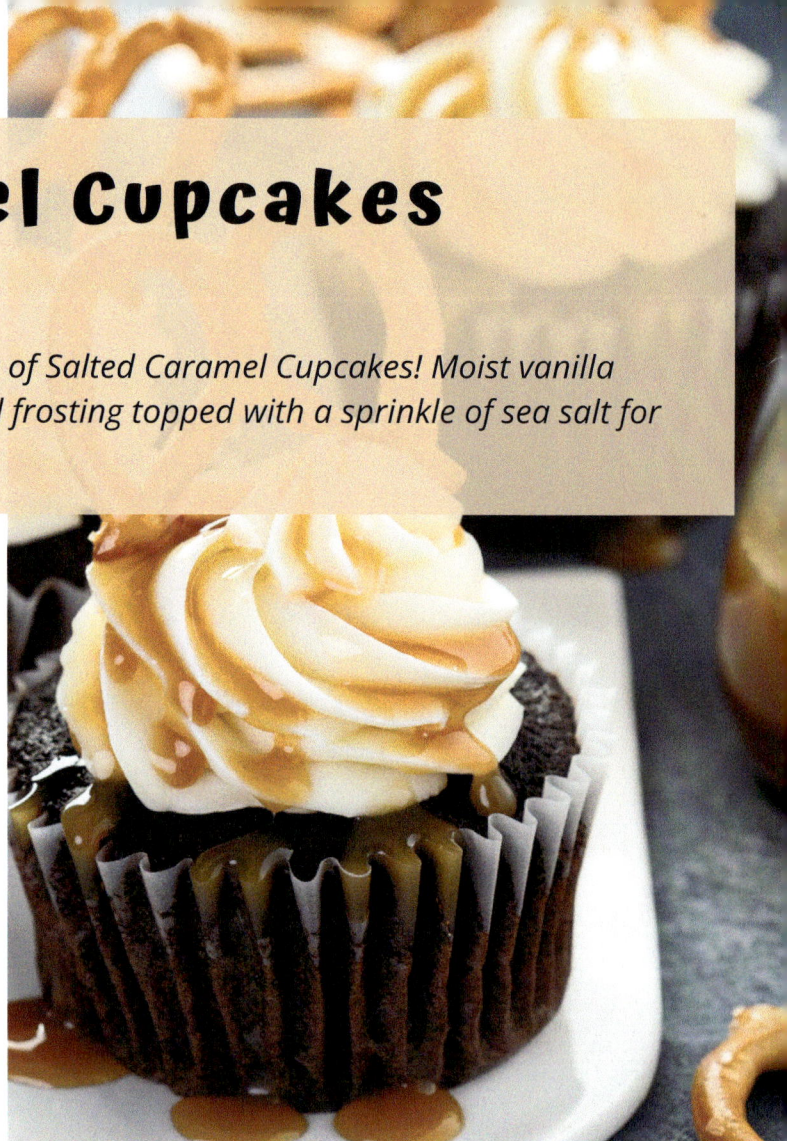

150g all-purpose flour

1 tsp baking powder

1/4 tsp salt

115g unsalted butter, softened

150g granulated sugar

2 large eggs

1 tsp vanilla extract

120ml milk

100g caramel sauce

Sea salt flakes

Method

- Preheat oven to 180°C (350°F) and line a 12-cup muffin tin with paper liners.
- In a medium bowl, whisk flour, baking powder, and salt.
- In a large bowl, cream butter and sugar until light and fluffy.
- Add eggs one at a time, mixing well after each addition.
- Stir in vanilla extract.
- Gradually add dry ingredients to wet ingredients, alternating with milk, mixing until just combined.
- Spoon a teaspoon of caramel sauce into each liner and top with cupcake batter until two-thirds full.
- Bake for 18-20 minutes or until a skewer comes out clean.
- Let cupcakes cool in tin, then transfer to wire rack to cool completely.
- Drizzle remaining caramel sauce over cupcakes and sprinkle with sea salt flakes.
- Enjoy salted caramel cupcakes!

Funfetti Cupcakes

🕐 **25 minutes**

Funfetti cupcakes are a colourful and fun dessert perfect for celebrations. These vanilla cupcakes are studded with rainbow sprinkles and topped with a fluffy buttercream frosting.

Ingredients

150g all-purpose flour
1 tsp baking powder
1/4 tsp salt
115g unsalted butter, softened
150g granulated sugar
2 large eggs
1 tsp vanilla extract
120ml milk
50g rainbow sprinkles

Method

- Preheat oven to 180°C (350°F) and line a 12-cup muffin tin with paper liners.
- Whisk flour, baking powder, and salt in a medium bowl.
- Cream softened butter and granulated sugar in a large mixing bowl with an electric mixer or wooden spoon until light and fluffy.
- Add eggs one at a time, mixing well after each addition, and stir in vanilla extract.
- Gradually add dry ingredients to wet ingredients, alternating with milk, and mix until just combined. Fold in rainbow sprinkles.
- Pour batter into lined muffin tin, filling each liner about two-thirds full.
- Bake for 18-20 minutes or until a skewer comes out clean when inserted in the center.
- Cool cupcakes in the tin for a few minutes, then transfer to a wire rack to cool completely. Frost and decorate cupcakes as desired.
- Enjoy your funfetti cupcakes!

Quick Bread Bliss

Savoury and Sweet Loaves to Love

Quick breads are a delicious and easy way to bake bread without the need for yeast or a long rising time. In this chapter, we will explore a variety of savoury and sweet quick bread recipes that you can whip up in no time. From classic banana bread to savoury cheese and herb loaves, there's a quick bread recipe for every taste bud.

Classic Banana Bread

🕐 **60 minutes**

Moist and flavourful, this classic banana bread is made with ripe bananas, butter, sugar, eggs, and flour. Perfect for breakfast, snack, or dessert, and easy to make.

Ingredients

2 ripe bananas, mashed

120g unsalted butter, softened

150g granulated sugar

2 large eggs

1 tsp vanilla extract

180g all-purpose flour

1 tsp baking powder

1/2 tsp baking soda

1/2 tsp salt

Method

- Preheat your oven to 180°C (350°F). Grease a 9x5 inch loaf pan with butter or cooking spray.
- In a large mixing bowl, cream the softened butter and granulated sugar together until light and fluffy, using an electric mixer or a wooden spoon.
- Add the eggs one at a time, mixing well after each addition.
- Stir in the mashed bananas and vanilla extract until evenly distributed.
- In a separate medium bowl, whisk together the all-purpose flour, baking powder, baking soda, and salt.
- Gradually add the dry ingredients to the wet ingredients, mixing until just combined.
- Pour the banana bread batter into the greased loaf pan.
- Bake the banana bread in the preheated oven for 50-60 minutes, or until a skewer inserted into the center comes out clean.
- Remove the banana bread from the oven and let it cool in the loaf pan for 10-15 minutes. Then, transfer it to a wire rack to cool completely.
- Once the banana bread is cool, slice it and serve. Enjoy your classic banana bread!

Savoury Cheddar & Herb Loaf

🕐 **60 minutes**

This savoury cheddar and herb loaf is perfect for brunch or as a side dish. The combination of cheddar cheese and herbs make this a flavourful and delicious treat.

Ingredients

300g all-purpose flour
2 tsp baking powder
1/2 tsp baking soda
1 tsp salt
1 tsp dried thyme
1 tsp dried basil
1 tsp dried oregano
50g unsalted butter, softened
200g sharp cheddar cheese, grated
2 large eggs
240ml milk

Method

- Preheat your oven to 180°C (350°F).
- Grease a 9x5 inch loaf pan. In a large mixing bowl, whisk together the dry ingredients including all-purpose flour, baking powder, baking soda, salt, dried thyme, dried basil, and dried oregano.
- In a separate medium bowl, cream softened butter and grated cheddar cheese. Add eggs one at a time, mixing well after each addition.
- Gradually add the dry ingredients to the wet ingredients, alternating with the milk, mixing until just combined.
- Pour batter into the greased loaf pan.
- Bake for 45-50 minutes, until the center is clean. Cool in the loaf pan for 10-15 minutes, then transfer it to a wire rack to cool completely. Serve sliced.

Sweet Cinnamon Swirl Bread

🕐 **60 minutes**

Indulge in the delicious aroma of freshly baked Sweet Cinnamon Swirl Bread. This fluffy and tender loaf is swirled with cinnamon and sugar, making it the perfect treat for any time of day.

Ingredients

For the bread:
375g all-purpose flour
1 tsp salt
50g unsalted butter, softened
1 large egg
240ml milk
75g granulated sugar
2 1/4 tsp active dry yeast

For the cinnamon swirl:
50g unsalted butter, melted
50g granulated sugar
1 tbsp ground cinnamon

Method

- Combine flour, salt, butter, egg, milk, sugar, and yeast in a large mixing bowl to make a soft dough.
- Knead on a floured surface until smooth.
- Place the dough in a greased bowl, cover, and let rise for 1 hour.
- Preheat oven to 180°C and grease a 9x5 inch loaf pan.
- Mix melted butter, sugar, and cinnamon in a small bowl to make the swirl.
- Roll out dough into 12x8 inch rectangle, spread cinnamon swirl, and roll tightly.
- Place in loaf pan, let rise for 30 minutes.
- Bake for 30-35 minutes and let cool before slicing and serving.

Parmesan & Sun-Dried Tomato Bread

🕐 **40 minutes**

Savoury Parmesan and sun-dried tomato bread, a delicious addition to any meal or a perfect snack on its own.

Ingredients

300g all-purpose flour
1 tsp salt
1 tsp sugar
2 tsp active dry yeast
240ml warm water
2 tbsp olive oil
50g grated Parmesan cheese
1/2 cup chopped sun-dried tomatoes
2 tbsp chopped fresh basil
1 tsp garlic powder

Method

- In a large mixing bowl, combine the all-purpose flour, salt, sugar, and active dry yeast. Mix well.
- Add the warm water and olive oil to the dry ingredients and mix until a soft dough forms.
- Knead the dough on a floured surface for 5-7 minutes, until smooth and elastic.
- Place the dough in a greased bowl, cover with a damp towel, and let it rise in a warm place for 1 hour, or until doubled in size.
- Preheat your oven to 180°C (350°F). Grease a 9x5 inch loaf pan with butter or cooking spray.
- In a small bowl, mix together the grated Parmesan cheese, chopped sun-dried tomatoes, chopped fresh basil, and garlic powder.
- Roll out the risen dough into a rectangle on a floured surface, approximately 12x8 inches.
- Spread the Parmesan and sun-dried tomato mixture evenly over the surface of the dough.
- Roll the dough up tightly into a log, starting from the long end.

Method

- Place the Parmesan and sun-dried tomato dough log into the greased loaf pan and let it rise again for 30 minutes.
- Bake the bread in the preheated oven for 30-35 minutes, or until the crust is golden brown and the bread sounds hollow when tapped.
- Remove the bread from the oven and let it cool in the loaf pan for 10-15 minutes. Then, transfer it to a wire rack to cool completely.
- Once the bread is cool, slice it and serve. Enjoy your Parmesan and sun-dried tomato bread!

Savoury Cheddar & Herb Loaf

🕐 **60 minutes**

A delicious savoury cheddar and herb loaf that is perfect for breakfast or as a side to any meal.

Ingredients

300g all-purpose flour

2 tsp baking powder

1/2 tsp baking soda

1 tsp salt

1 tsp dried thyme

1 tsp dried basil

1 tsp dried oregano

50g unsalted butter, softened

200g sharp cheddar cheese, grated

2 large eggs

240ml milk

Method

- Preheat oven to 180°C (350°F) and grease a 9x5 inch loaf pan.
- Mix flour, baking powder, baking soda, salt, thyme, basil, and oregano in a large bowl.
- In a separate bowl, combine softened butter and grated cheddar cheese.
- Add eggs one at a time.
- Gradually add dry ingredients and milk to the wet mixture. Pour into loaf pan.
- Bake for 45-50 minutes at 180°C (350°F).
- Cool in pan for 10-15 minutes then transfer to wire rack to cool completely.
- Slice and serve.

Zucchini and Parmesan Bread

🕐 **60 minutes**

This Zucchini and Parmesan Bread is a savoury and delicious twist on traditional bread, featuring the subtle flavour of zucchini and the sharpness of Parmesan cheese.

Ingredients

250g all-purpose flour
2 tsp baking powder
1 tsp salt
1/2 tsp black pepper
2 large eggs
120ml milk
80ml vegetable oil
1 medium zucchini, grated and squeezed dry
100g grated Parmesan cheese
2 tbsp chopped fresh parsley

Method

- Preheat your oven to 180°C (350°F). Grease a 9x5 inch loaf pan with butter or cooking spray.
- In a large mixing bowl, whisk together the all-purpose flour, baking powder, salt, and black pepper.
- In a separate medium bowl, whisk together the eggs, milk, and vegetable oil until well combined.
- Add the grated zucchini, grated Parmesan cheese, and chopped fresh parsley to the wet ingredients, mixing until evenly distributed.
- Gradually add the wet ingredients to the dry ingredients, mixing until just combined.
- Pour the zucchini and Parmesan bread batter into the greased loaf pan.
- Bake the bread in the preheated oven for 45-50 minutes, or until a skewer inserted into the center comes out clean.
- Remove the bread from the oven and let it cool in the pan for 10-15 minutes. Then, transfer it to a wire rack to cool completely.
- Once the bread is cool, slice it and serve. Enjoy your zucchini and Parmesan bread!

Speedy Snack Bars
Nutritious Baked Bites for On-the-Go Teens

Each of these recipes can be customized with your favorite nuts, dried fruits, or chocolate chips to create your own unique snack bars. Perfect for busy teenagers who need a quick and nutritious snack on-the-go!

Peanut Butter and Jelly Bars

🕐 **30 minutes**

Sweet and tangy strawberry jam is sandwiched between layers of creamy peanut butter goodness.

Ingredients

150g all-purpose flour

100g rolled oats

100g brown sugar

1 tsp baking powder

1/2 tsp salt

120g unsalted butter, melted

240g creamy peanut butter

120ml milk

1 large egg

200g strawberry jam or jelly

Method

- Preheat oven to 180°C (350°F) and grease a 9x13 inch baking dish.
- In a bowl, mix all-purpose flour, rolled oats, brown sugar, baking powder, and salt.
- Add melted unsalted butter, creamy peanut butter, milk, and egg, then combine.
- Press 2/3 of the mixture into the baking dish, spread jam over it, then add remaining mixture by spoonfuls.
- Bake for 25-30 minutes or until golden brown.
- Cool for 10-15 minutes, then transfer to a wire rack to cool completely.
- Slice and serve.

No-Bake Granola Bars

🕐 **10 minutes**

No-Bake Granola Bars are a quick and easy snack made with oats, honey, and peanut butter. Perfect for a healthy, on-the-go breakfast or snack.

Ingredients

240g rolled oats
80g chopped nuts (such as almonds, pecans, or walnuts)
80g chopped dried fruit (such as cranberries or raisins)
40g shredded coconut
60g honey
60g peanut butter
40g unsalted butter
1 tsp vanilla extract

Method

- Line an 8x8 inch square baking dish with parchment paper.
- In a large mixing bowl, combine the rolled oats, chopped nuts, chopped dried fruit, and shredded coconut.
- In a separate medium bowl, heat the honey, peanut butter, unsalted butter, and vanilla extract in the microwave or on the stove until the mixture is smooth and well combined.
- Pour the honey and peanut butter mixture over the dry ingredients and mix until everything is evenly coated.
- Press the mixture firmly and evenly into the prepared baking dish.
- Chill the granola bars in the refrigerator for at least 2 hours, or until firm.
- Once chilled, remove the granola bars from the baking dish and cut them into bars.
- Serve the granola bars immediately or store them in an airtight container in the refrigerator for up to one week.

Almond Cranberry Bars

🕐 **30 minutes**

Almond Cranberry Bars are a delicious combination of tart cranberries and crunchy almonds, baked into a chewy bar that's perfect for snacking on the go or as a dessert.

Ingredients

200g all-purpose flour
100g rolled oats
80g sliced almonds
80g dried cranberries
1/2 tsp baking soda
1/2 tsp salt
120g unsalted butter, softened
150g brown sugar
1 large egg
1 tsp vanilla extract

Method

- Preheat your oven to 180°C (350°F). Grease a 9x13 inch baking dish with butter or cooking spray.
- In a large mixing bowl, combine the all-purpose flour, rolled oats, sliced almonds, dried cranberries, baking soda, and salt.
- In a separate large mixing bowl, cream together the softened unsalted butter and brown sugar until light and fluffy.
- Add the egg and vanilla extract to the butter and sugar mixture and beat until well combined.
- Gradually add the dry ingredients to the wet ingredients, mixing until just combined.
- Press the mixture firmly and evenly into the prepared baking dish.
- Bake the bars in the preheated oven for 25-30 minutes, or until golden brown.
- Remove the bars from the oven and let them cool in the baking dish for 10-15 minutes. Then, transfer them to a wire rack to cool completely.
- Once the bars are cool, slice them into bars and serve. Enjoy your almond cranberry bars!

Oatmeal Raisin Bars

🕐 **30 minutes**

These Oatmeal Raisin Bars are chewy and sweet. Perfect for a snack or breakfast on-the-go, they're easy to make and deliciously satisfying.

Ingredients

200g all-purpose flour
150g rolled oats
1 tsp baking soda
1/2 tsp salt
120g unsalted butter, softened
150g brown sugar
2 large eggs
1 tsp vanilla extract
150g raisins

Method

- Preheat your oven to 180°C (350°F). Grease a 9x13 inch baking dish with butter or cooking spray.
- In a medium mixing bowl, whisk together the all-purpose flour, rolled oats, baking soda, and salt.
- In a separate large mixing bowl, cream together the softened unsalted butter and brown sugar until light and fluffy.
- Add the eggs and vanilla extract to the butter and sugar mixture and beat until well combined.
- Gradually add the dry ingredients to the wet ingredients, mixing until just combined.
- Fold in the raisins.
- Pour the batter into the prepared baking dish and smooth it out into an even layer.
- Bake the bars in the preheated oven for 25-30 minutes, or until golden brown.
- Remove the bars from the oven and let them cool in the baking dish for 10-15 minutes. Then, transfer them to a wire rack to cool completely.
- Once the bars are cool, slice them into bars and serve. Enjoy your oatmeal raisin bars!

Apple Cinnamon Bars

🕐 **30 minutes**

Apple Cinnamon Bars are a delicious dessert made with grated apples and warm spices, like cinnamon and nutmeg. Perfect for a fall treat or anytime snack.

Ingredients

200g all-purpose flour
1 tsp baking powder
1/2 tsp salt
1 tsp ground cinnamon
120g unsalted butter, softened
150g granulated sugar
2 large eggs
1 tsp vanilla extract
2 medium apples, peeled and grated
80g chopped walnuts (optional)

Method

- Preheat oven to 180°C (350°F). Grease a 9x13 inch baking dish.
- In a medium mixing bowl, whisk together flour, baking powder, salt, and cinnamon.
- Cream softened butter and sugar in a separate large mixing bowl.
- Add eggs and vanilla extract and beat until well combined.
- Gradually add the dry ingredients to the wet ingredients, mix until just combined.
- Fold in grated apples and chopped walnuts (if using).
- Pour batter into the prepared dish and smooth into an even layer.
- Bake bars for 30-35 minutes, or until a skewer comes out clean.
- Cool for 10-15 minutes, then transfer to a wire rack to cool completely.
- Slice bars and serve.

Pancakes & Waffles

Fast and Fabulous Breakfast Treats

Who doesn't love waking up to a stack of warm pancakes or crispy waffles for breakfast? In this chapter, we've got you covered with quick and easy recipes for delicious pancakes and waffles that are perfect for busy mornings.

Classic Buttermilk Pancakes

🕐 **10 minutes**

Fluffy and golden brown, these classic buttermilk pancakes are the perfect breakfast treat. Serve with butter and maple syrup for a delicious start to your day.

Ingredients

200g all-purpose flour

2 tbsp granulated sugar

2 tsp baking powder

1/2 tsp baking soda

1/2 tsp salt

350ml buttermilk

1 large egg

2 tbsp unsalted butter, melted

1 tsp vanilla extract

Butter or oil, for greasing the pan

Method

- In a large mixing bowl, whisk together the flour, sugar, baking powder, baking soda, and salt.
- In a separate medium mixing bowl, whisk together the buttermilk, egg, melted unsalted butter, and vanilla extract.
- Add the wet ingredients to the dry ingredients and stir until just combined. Do not overmix the batter, as this can result in tough pancakes.
- Heat a non-stick skillet or griddle over medium-high heat. Grease the pan with butter or oil.
- Using a 1/4 cup measure, pour the batter onto the hot pan. Cook the pancakes for 2-3 minutes on each side, or until golden brown and cooked through.
- Repeat with the remaining batter, greasing the pan as needed.
- Serve the pancakes warm with your favorite toppings, such as maple syrup, whipped cream, fresh fruit, or chocolate chips. Enjoy your classic buttermilk pancakes!

Blueberry Pancakes

🕐 **10 minutes**

Blueberry pancakes are a classic breakfast treat, bursting with juicy blueberries in fluffy batter. Topped with butter and syrup, they make a delicious start to your day.

Ingredients

200g all-purpose flour
1 tsp baking powder
1/2 tsp salt
1 tsp ground cinnamon
120g unsalted butter, softened
150g granulated sugar
2 large eggs
1 tsp vanilla extract
2 medium apples, peeled and grated
80g chopped walnuts (optional)

Method

- In a large mixing bowl, whisk together the flour, sugar, baking powder, baking soda, and salt.
- In a separate medium mixing bowl, whisk together the buttermilk, egg, melted unsalted butter, and vanilla extract.
- Add the wet ingredients to the dry ingredients and stir until just combined. Do not overmix the batter, as this can result in tough pancakes.
- Gently fold in the fresh blueberries.
- Heat a non-stick skillet or griddle over medium-high heat. Grease the pan with butter or oil.
- Using a 1/4 cup measure, pour the batter onto the hot pan. Cook the pancakes for 2-3 minutes on each side, or until golden brown and cooked through.
- Repeat with the remaining batter, greasing the pan as needed.
- Serve the pancakes warm with additional fresh blueberries and your favorite toppings, such as maple syrup, whipped cream, or honey. Enjoy your blueberry pancakes!

Savoury Cheese & Herb Waffles

🕐 **10 minutes**

These savoury waffles are made with cheese and herbs, making them a tasty and satisfying breakfast or brunch option. Perfect when topped with a poached egg or some bacon.

Ingredients

2 cups all-purpose flour
2 tbsp granulated sugar
2 tsp baking powder
1/2 tsp baking soda
1/2 tsp salt
1 1/2 cups buttermilk
2 large eggs
1/3 cup unsalted butter, melted and cooled
1 tsp dried thyme
1 tsp dried oregano
1/2 tsp garlic powder
1/2 cup grated cheddar cheese
1/4 cup chopped fresh chives

Method

- In a large mixing bowl, whisk together the flour, granulated sugar, baking powder, baking soda, and salt.
- In a separate medium mixing bowl, whisk together the buttermilk, eggs, melted unsalted butter, dried thyme, dried oregano, and garlic powder.
- Add the wet ingredients to the dry ingredients and stir until just combined. Do not overmix the batter, as this can result in tough waffles.
- Fold in the grated cheddar cheese and chopped fresh chives.
- Preheat your waffle maker according to its instructions.
- Pour enough waffle batter into the waffle maker to cover the surface, and close the lid. Cook the waffles until golden brown and crisp, usually about 4-5 minutes.
- Repeat with the remaining batter, greasing the waffle maker as needed.
- Serve the waffles warm with additional grated cheese and fresh chives on top. Enjoy your savoury cheese and herb waffles!

Fluffy Belgian Waffles

🕐 **10 minutes**

These Fluffy Belgian Waffles are a breakfast delight! Crispy on the outside, fluffy on the inside. Perfect with syrup, whipped cream and fresh fruit.

Ingredients

250g all-purpose flour
2 tbsp granulated sugar
2 tsp baking powder
1/2 tsp baking soda
1/2 tsp salt
350ml buttermilk
2 large eggs, separated
4 tbsp unsalted butter, melted and cooled
1 tsp vanilla extract

Method

- In a large mixing bowl, whisk together the flour, sugar, baking powder, baking soda, and salt.
- In a separate medium mixing bowl, whisk together the buttermilk, egg yolks, melted unsalted butter, and vanilla extract.
- Add the wet ingredients to the dry ingredients and stir until just combined. Do not overmix the batter, as this can result in tough waffles.
- In another mixing bowl, whisk the egg whites until stiff peaks form.
- Gently fold the egg whites into the batter, being careful not to deflate them.
- Preheat your waffle maker according to its instructions.
- Pour enough batter into the waffle maker to cover the surface, and close the lid. Cook the waffles until golden brown and crisp, usually about 4-5 minutes.
- Repeat with the remaining batter, greasing the waffle maker as needed.
- Serve the waffles warm with your favorite toppings, such as fresh fruit, whipped cream, chocolate chips, or syrup. Enjoy your fluffy Belgian waffles!

Chocolate Chip Pancakes

🕐 **10 minutes**

Indulge in fluffy Chocolate Chip Pancakes, loaded with chocolate chips that melt in your mouth with every bite. Perfect for a sweet and satisfying breakfast treat!

Ingredients

200g all-purpose flour
2 tbsp granulated sugar
2 tsp baking powder
1/2 tsp baking soda
1/2 tsp salt
350ml buttermilk
1 large egg
2 tbsp unsalted butter, melted
1 tsp vanilla extract
100g chocolate chips
Butter or oil, for greasing the pan

Method

- In a large mixing bowl, whisk together the flour, sugar, baking powder, baking soda, and salt.
- In a separate medium mixing bowl, whisk together the buttermilk, egg, melted unsalted butter, and vanilla extract.
- Add the wet ingredients to the dry ingredients and stir until just combined. Do not overmix the batter, as this can result in tough pancakes.
- Gently fold in the chocolate chips.
- Heat a non-stick skillet or griddle over medium-high heat. Grease the pan with butter or oil.
- Using a 1/4 cup measure, pour the batter onto the hot pan. Cook the pancakes for 2-3 minutes on each side, or until golden brown and cooked through.
- Repeat with the remaining batter, greasing the pan as needed.
- Serve the pancakes warm with additional chocolate chips and your favourite toppings, such as whipped cream, berries, or maple syrup. Enjoy your chocolate chip pancakes!

Time-Saving Tips

Baking Hacks for Busy Teen Bakers

In this chapter, we'll share some handy tips and tricks for saving time in the kitchen. These baking hacks will help you whip up delicious treats in no time, without sacrificing flavour or quality. From using shortcuts to clever techniques, these hacks will make baking easier, faster, and more fun.

Quick and Easy Mug Cake

🕐 **3 minutes**

Indulge in a warm and delicious dessert in just minutes with a quick and easy mug cake. Perfect for satisfying your sweet cravings in a pinch.

Ingredients

4 tbsp all-purpose flour
2 tbsp granulated sugar
2 tbsp unsweetened cocoa powder
1/4 tsp baking powder
3 tbsp milk
2 tbsp vegetable oil
1/4 tsp vanilla extract
Pinch of salt
1 tbsp chocolate chips (optional)

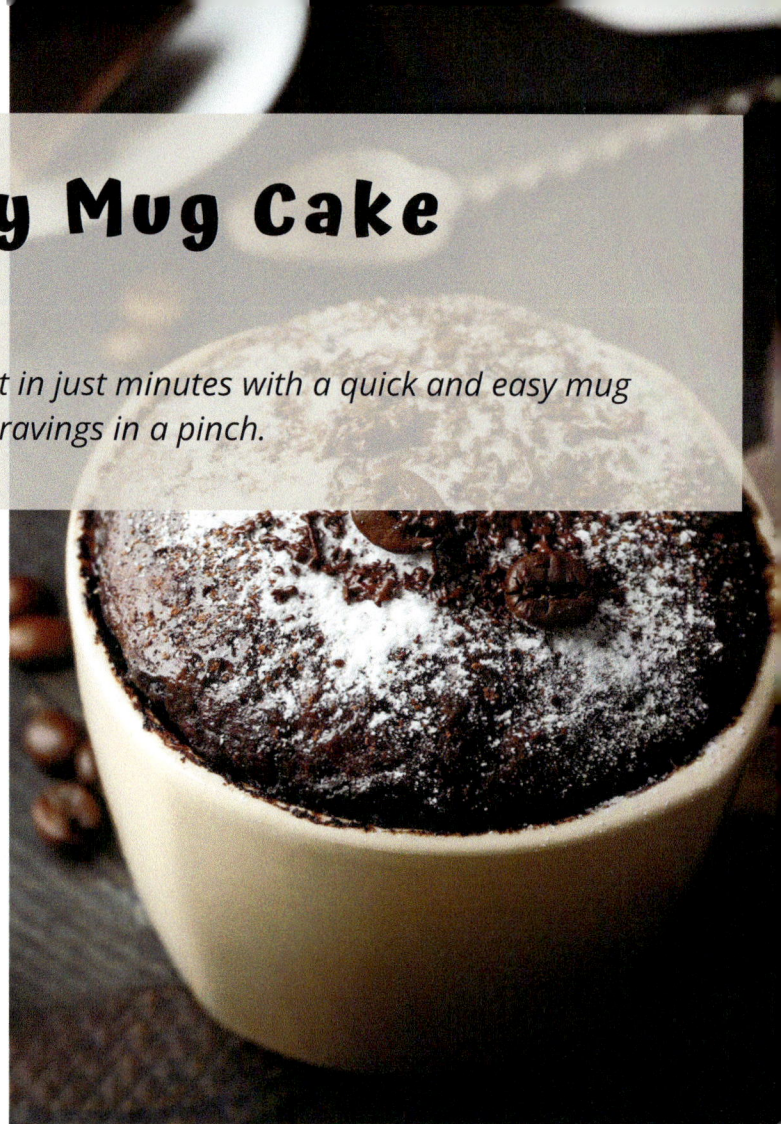

Method

- In a microwave-safe mug, whisk together the flour, sugar, cocoa powder, baking powder, and salt until well combined.
- Add the milk, vegetable oil, and vanilla extract to the mug, and stir until the batter is smooth and no lumps remain.
- Fold in the chocolate chips, if using.
- Microwave the mug cake on high for 1 minute and 30 seconds, or until the cake has risen and is cooked through.
- Let the mug cake cool for a few minutes before serving. Enjoy your quick and easy mug cake!

One-Bowl Chocolate Chip Cookies

🕐 **15 minutes**

These one-bowl chocolate chip cookies are quick and easy to make, with a soft and chewy texture and plenty of melty chocolate chips in every bite.

Ingredients

2 1/4 cups all-purpose flour
1 tsp baking soda
1 tsp salt
1 cup unsalted butter, melted and cooled
1 cup brown sugar
1/2 cup granulated sugar
2 large eggs
2 tsp vanilla extract
2 cups chocolate chips

Method

- Preheat your oven to 375°F (190°C).
- In a large mixing bowl, whisk together the flour, baking soda, and salt.
- Add the melted and cooled unsalted butter, brown sugar, granulated sugar, eggs, and vanilla extract to the bowl, and stir until the batter is smooth and well combined.
- Fold in the chocolate chips until they are evenly distributed throughout the batter.
- Using a spoon or cookie scoop, drop spoonfuls of the cookie dough onto a lined baking sheet, leaving about 2 inches of space between each cookie.
- Bake the cookies in the preheated oven for 12-15 minutes, or until they are golden brown and set around the edges.
- Let the cookies cool on the baking sheet for a few minutes before transferring them to a wire rack to cool completely. Enjoy your one-bowl chocolate chip cookies!

Speedy Pizza Dough

🕐 **15 minutes**

Make homemade pizza in a snap with this Speedy Pizza Dough recipe. With just a few simple ingredients and 30 minutes, you'll have a delicious pizza crust ready to top with your favourite ingredients.

Ingredients

2 cups all-purpose flour
1 tbsp baking powder
1 tsp salt
1/2 tsp garlic powder
1/4 tsp dried oregano
1/4 tsp dried basil
2/3 cup warm water
1/4 cup olive oil

Method

- Preheat your oven to 425°F (220°C).
- In a large mixing bowl, whisk together the flour, baking powder, salt, garlic powder, dried oregano, and dried basil.
- Add the warm water and olive oil to the bowl, and stir until the dough comes together into a ball.
- Turn the dough out onto a floured surface, and knead it for about 5 minutes until it becomes smooth and elastic.
- Roll the dough out into your desired pizza shape, and transfer it to a greased baking sheet or pizza stone.
- Add your desired toppings to the pizza.
- Bake the pizza in the preheated oven for 12-15 minutes, or until the crust is golden brown and the cheese is melted and bubbly.
- Remove the pizza from the oven, let it cool for a few minutes, and slice it up to serve. Enjoy your speedy pizza!

3-Ingredient Peanut Butter Cookies

🕐 **10 minutes**

These 3-ingredient peanut butter cookies are a quick and easy treat that's perfect for any occasion. They're soft, chewy, and packed with peanut butter flavour.

Ingredients

1 cup creamy peanut butter
1 cup granulated sugar
1 large egg

Method

- Preheat your oven to 350°F (175°C).
- In a large mixing bowl, stir together the peanut butter, granulated sugar, and egg until the batter is smooth and well combined.
- Using a spoon or cookie scoop, drop spoonfuls of the cookie dough onto a lined baking sheet, leaving about 2 inches of space between each cookie.
- Using a fork, press down gently on each cookie to create a criss-cross pattern on the surface.
- Bake the cookies in the preheated oven for 10-12 minutes, or until they are golden brown and set around the edges.
- Let the cookies cool on the baking sheet for a few minutes before transferring them to a wire rack to cool completely. Enjoy your 3-ingredient peanut butter cookies!

5-Minute Homemade Whipped Cream

🕐 **15 minutes**

Make perfect whipped cream in just 5 minutes with this easy homemade recipe! All you need is heavy cream, sugar, and vanilla extract for a delicious topping for desserts.

Ingredients

- 1 cup heavy cream
- 2 tbsp granulated sugar
- 1 tsp vanilla extract

Method

- Chill a large mixing bowl and whisk in the freezer for at least 15 minutes before starting.
- Pour the heavy cream, sugar, and vanilla extract into the chilled bowl.
- Using a hand mixer or a stand mixer with the whisk attachment, beat the mixture on high speed for 2-3 minutes, or until soft peaks form.
- Be careful not to over-whip the cream, as it can turn into butter. Stop beating once the cream holds its shape and has a smooth and creamy texture.
- Use the whipped cream immediately, or store it in the refrigerator until ready to use. It will keep well for up to 2-3 days.
- Serve the whipped cream on top of your favorite desserts, such as pies, cakes, fruits, or use it to frost cupcakes. Enjoy your delicious homemade whipped cream in just 5 minutes!

Make-Ahead Magic

Prepping Your Ingredients for Stress-Free Baking

In this chapter, we'll share some handy tips and tricks for saving time in the kitchen. These baking hacks will help you whip up delicious treats in no time, without sacrificing flavour or quality. From using shortcuts to clever techniques, these hacks will make baking easier, faster, and more fun.

Freezer-Friendly Pie Crust:

🕐 **10 minutes**

Make pie baking a breeze with this freezer-friendly pie crust. It's easy to prepare and can be stored in the freezer for whenever you need a quick and delicious crust.

Ingredients

2 1/2 cups all-purpose flour
1 tsp salt
1 tbsp granulated sugar
1 cup (2 sticks) unsalted butter, cut into small pieces and chilled
1/4 - 1/2 cup ice water

Method

- In a large mixing bowl, whisk together the flour, salt, and sugar.
- Using a pastry cutter or your fingers, cut in the chilled butter until the mixture resembles coarse crumbs with some larger pieces of butter.
- Drizzle 1/4 cup of ice water over the flour mixture and stir with a fork until the dough starts to come together. Add more water as needed, a tablespoon at a time, until the dough is moist but not wet.
- Turn the dough out onto a lightly floured surface and shape it into a ball. Divide the ball into two equal parts and shape each half into a flat disk.
- Wrap each disk tightly in plastic wrap and refrigerate for at least 1 hour or up to 2 days.
- If you plan to freeze the dough, wrap each disk in plastic wrap and then aluminum foil, and freeze for up to 3 months.
- When ready to use, remove the dough from the refrigerator or freezer and let it sit at room temperature for 10-15 minutes to soften slightly.
- Roll out the dough on a lightly floured surface to the desired thickness and size. Use the dough to line a pie dish and add your desired filling.

Method

- If using frozen dough, let it thaw in the refrigerator overnight before rolling it out.
- To blind bake the crust, preheat your oven to 375°F (190°C). Line the crust with parchment paper and fill it with pie weights or dried beans. Bake for 20-25 minutes or until lightly golden brown. Remove the weights and parchment paper and continue baking for an additional 10-15 minutes until the crust is golden brown all over.
- Let the pie crust cool completely before filling it with your desired filling.

Make-Ahead Pizza Sauce

🕐 **30 minutes**

Make-Ahead Pizza Sauce: A flavourful blend of tomatoes, herbs, and spices that can be made in advance and stored in the fridge or freezer for quick and easy pizza nights.

Ingredients

1 can (28 oz) crushed tomatoes
2 cloves garlic, minced
1 tsp dried oregano
1 tsp dried basil
1/2 tsp salt
1/4 tsp black pepper
1 tbsp olive oil

Method

- In a large mixing bowl, combine the crushed tomatoes, garlic, oregano, basil, salt, black pepper, and olive oil. Stir until well combined.
- Transfer the mixture to a blender or food processor and puree until smooth.
- Pour the sauce into a large saucepan and bring it to a simmer over medium heat.
- Reduce the heat to low and simmer the sauce, stirring occasionally, for about 15-20 minutes or until it has thickened slightly.
- Remove the saucepan from the heat and let the sauce cool to room temperature.
- Once the sauce has cooled, transfer it to a sealable container or jar and refrigerate for up to 1 week or freeze for up to 3 months.
- When you're ready to use the sauce, simply remove it from the refrigerator or freezer and let it come to room temperature before spreading it on your pizza crust.

*Note: This recipe makes about 2 cups of pizza sauce. If you prefer a spicier sauce, you can add some crushed red pepper flakes to the mixture.

132

Freezer-friendly Homemade Pesto

🕐 **10 minutes**

This freezer-friendly homemade pesto is bursting with flavour and is perfect for adding to pasta, sandwiches, or as a dip. Make it ahead and enjoy it anytime!

Ingredients

2 cups fresh basil leaves, packed
1/2 cup grated Parmesan cheese
1/2 cup extra-virgin olive oil
1/3 cup pine nuts
3 garlic cloves, minced
1/4 tsp salt
1/4 tsp black pepper

Method

- Rinse the basil leaves and pat them dry with a paper towel. Remove the stems and discard them.
- In a food processor, combine the basil leaves, Parmesan cheese, olive oil, pine nuts, garlic, salt, and black pepper.
- Pulse the mixture until it is smooth and well combined.
- Transfer the pesto to a sealable container or jar.
- If you want to freeze the pesto, cover the container tightly with plastic wrap, pressing the wrap directly onto the surface of the pesto to prevent air from getting in. Then, cover the container with a lid and freeze for up to 3 months.
- If you want to use the pesto immediately, you can store it in the refrigerator for up to 1 week.

*You can use this pesto as a spread on sandwiches, as a dip for vegetables, or as a sauce for pasta dishes. To thaw frozen pesto, simply transfer it to the refrigerator and let it thaw overnight.

Pre-Made Pancake Mix

🕐 **30 minutes**

Our pre-made pancake mix makes breakfast easy and delicious. Simply add water or milk, mix, and cook up fluffy and satisfying pancakes in minutes.

Ingredients

6 cups all-purpose flour
1 1/2 cups dry milk powder
1/4 cup granulated sugar
3 tbsp baking powder
1 tbsp baking soda
1 tbsp salt

Method

- In a large mixing bowl, combine the all-purpose flour, dry milk powder, granulated sugar, baking powder, baking soda, and salt.
- Stir the ingredients until they are well combined.
- Transfer the pancake mix to an airtight container or a sealable plastic bag.
- Label the container or bag with the date and the type of mix (i.e. "Pancake Mix").
- Store the pancake mix in a cool, dry place for up to 3 months.

To make pancakes:
- In a mixing bowl, combine 1 1/2 cups of pancake mix, 1 egg, and 1 cup of water.
- Whisk the ingredients together until they are well combined.
- Heat a lightly oiled griddle or frying pan over medium-high heat.
- Pour about 1/4 cup of batter onto the griddle or frying pan for each pancake.
- Cook the pancakes for about 2-3 minutes on each side, or until they are golden brown.
- Serve the pancakes hot with your favourite toppings, such as butter, syrup, fresh fruit, or whipped cream.

Prepared Muffin Batter

🕐 **10 minutes**

Prepared muffin batter is a convenient and time-saving option for making fresh muffins quickly. Just scoop the batter into muffin tins and bake for a delicious breakfast or snack.

Ingredients

2 cups all-purpose flour
1/2 cup granulated sugar
1 tbsp baking powder
1/2 tsp salt
1/2 cup unsalted butter, melted and cooled
1 cup milk
2 large eggs, beaten
1 tsp vanilla extract
1 cup mix-ins (such as blueberries, chocolate chips, or chopped nuts)

Method

- In a large mixing bowl, whisk together the all-purpose flour, granulated sugar, baking powder, and salt.
- In a separate mixing bowl, whisk together the melted butter, milk, beaten eggs, and vanilla extract.
- Pour the wet ingredients into the dry ingredients and mix until just combined.
- Add in your desired mix-ins, such as blueberries, chocolate chips, or chopped nuts, and gently stir until evenly distributed throughout the batter.
- Transfer the prepared muffin batter to an airtight container or a sealable plastic bag.
- Label the container or bag with the date and the type of batter (i.e. "Muffin Batter").
- Store the muffin batter in the refrigerator for up to 2 days.

Method

To make muffins:

- Preheat your oven to 375°F (190°C).
- Line a muffin tin with paper liners or grease the muffin cups with cooking spray.
- Remove the prepared muffin batter from the refrigerator and give it a quick stir.
- Using a spoon or a cookie scoop, fill each muffin cup about 2/3 full with the muffin batter.
- Bake the muffins in the preheated oven for about 18-20 minutes, or until a toothpick inserted into the center of a muffin comes out clean.
- Remove the muffins from the oven and let them cool in the muffin tin for 5 minutes.
- Transfer the muffins to a wire rack and let them cool completely before serving.

Baking with Friends

Fun Group Baking Activities and Challenges

Baking with friends can be a delightful and memorable experience. It's a chance to gather together in the kitchen, share the joy of baking, and create delicious treats as a team. In this chapter, we'll explore some fun group baking activities and challenges that are perfect for baking with friends. Whether you're planning a bake-off, a baking challenge, or simply baking together for fun, these activities are sure to bring laughter, creativity, and friendly competition to your baking adventures.

These recipes are designed to be interactive and enjoyable, allowing you and your friends to work together, experiment with flavors and decorations, and create tasty treats to share and enjoy. So grab your aprons, gather your friends, and get ready for some baking fun with these group baking activities and challenges!

Chocolate Lava Cakes

🕐 **20 minutes**

Indulge in the rich, chocolatey goodness of these decadent chocolate lava cakes. With a warm, gooey center, they're the perfect dessert for any chocolate lover.

Ingredients

225g unsalted butter
225g semi-sweet chocolate, chopped
300g granulated sugar
4 large eggs, at room temperature
1 tsp pure vanilla extract
60ml espresso or strong brewed coffee, cooled
140g all-purpose flour
60g unsweetened cocoa powder
1/4 tsp salt
2 tsp instant espresso powder

Method

- Preheat your oven to 220°C (425°F) and grease six ramekins or custard cups with butter or cooking spray.
- In a microwave-safe bowl, melt the butter and chopped chocolate together in short intervals, stirring in between, until fully melted and smooth.
- In a separate mixing bowl, whisk together the sugar, eggs, vanilla extract, and cooled coffee until well combined.
- Gradually pour the melted chocolate mixture into the egg mixture, whisking constantly, until fully combined.
- Sift in the flour, cocoa powder, salt, and instant espresso powder into the chocolate mixture, and fold gently with a spatula until just incorporated.
- Divide the batter evenly among the prepared ramekins or custard cups.

Method

- Place the ramekins or custard cups onto a baking sheet and bake in the preheated oven for 12-14 minutes, or until the edges are set but the center is still slightly jiggly.
- Remove from the oven and let the lava cakes cool for 5 minutes before carefully running a knife along the edges and inverting them onto serving plates.
- Dust with powdered sugar, if desired, and serve immediately while still warm. The center should be gooey and molten.

*Note: You can also make the batter ahead of time and refrigerate it, then bake the lava cakes just before serving for a fresh and warm treat.

Berry Cobbler

🕐 **40 minutes**

This berry cobbler is a perfect dessert for summer with its juicy, sweet berries and a golden-brown biscuit-like topping. It's quick and easy to make, and always a crowd-pleaser.

Ingredients

2500g mixed berries (such as strawberries, blueberries, raspberries, and blackberries)
100g granulated sugar
1 tbsp cornstarch
1 tsp lemon juice
1 tsp vanilla extract
150g all-purpose flour
50g granulated sugar
1 tsp baking powder
1/4 tsp salt
100g unsalted butter, melted
125ml milk

Method

- Preheat your oven to 180°C (350°F) and grease a baking dish.
- In a mixing bowl, toss the mixed berries with 100g of sugar, cornstarch, lemon juice, and vanilla extract until well combined. Pour the berry mixture into the prepared baking dish.
- In another mixing bowl, whisk together the flour, 50g of sugar, baking powder, and salt.
- Stir in the melted butter and milk into the dry ingredients until just combined, being careful not to overmix.
- Drop spoonfuls of the batter evenly over the berry mixture in the baking dish.
- Bake in the preheated oven for 30-35 minutes, or until the topping is golden brown and the berry mixture is bubbling.
- Remove from the oven and let it cool for a few minutes before serving.
- Serve warm as is, or with a scoop of vanilla ice cream or a dollop of whipped cream for extra indulgence.

*Note: You can use any combination of fresh or frozen berries for this recipe, and adjust the sugar amount based on the sweetness of the berries and your personal preference.

Rainbow Cupcakes

🕐 **30 minutes**

Rainbow cupcakes are a colourful and fun treat that are perfect for any celebration! Made with vibrant layers of cake and topped with fluffy frosting and sprinkles.

Ingredients

200g unsalted butter, at room temperature
200g granulated sugar
4 large eggs
1 tsp vanilla extract
200g all-purpose flour
2 tsp baking powder
1/4 tsp salt
120ml milk
Food coloring (red, orange, yellow, green, blue, and purple)
Cupcake liners

For the Buttercream Frosting:
250g unsalted butter, at room temperature
500g powdered sugar
2 tsp vanilla extract
2-3 tbsp milk
Food colo ring (optional)

Method

- Preheat your oven to 180°C (350°F) and line a muffin tin with cupcake liners.
- In a large mixing bowl, cream the butter and sugar together until light and fluffy.
- Beat in the eggs, one at a time, then add the vanilla extract and mix until well combined.
- In a separate bowl, whisk together the flour, baking powder, and salt.
- Gradually add the dry ingredients to the wet ingredients, alternating with the milk, beginning and ending with the dry ingredients. Mix until just combined.
- Divide the batter equally into six bowls.
- Add a few drops of different food coloring to each bowl, one color per bowl, and stir until well combined to achieve a rainbow of colored batters.
- Starting with one color, drop spoonfuls of the batter into the center of each cupcake liner, then add the next color on top, continuing until all the colors have been used.
- Use a toothpick or skewer to swirl the colors gently, creating a marbled effect.
- Bake in the preheated oven for 18-20 minutes, or until a toothpick inserted into the center of a cupcake comes out clean.
- Remove from the oven and let the cupcakes cool completely before frosting.

Method

_____

For the Buttercream Frosting:
- In a large mixing bowl, beat the butter until creamy and smooth.
- Gradually add the powdered sugar, vanilla extract, and milk, and beat until light and fluffy.
- Optional: Divide the frosting into separate bowls and add a few drops of food coloring to each bowl, then stir until well combined to achieve different colored frostings.
- Once the cupcakes are completely cooled, frost them with the buttercream frosting using a piping bag or a butter knife.
- Decorate with additional rainbow-themed decorations, if desired.
- Serve and enjoy these colorful and delicious rainbow cupcakes with friends!
- Note: You can use gel or liquid food coloring for this recipe, but be sure to adjust the amount to achieve the desired intensity of colors. You can also use different frosting techniques to create unique designs with the rainbow colors, such as a rainbow swirl or a rainbow rosette.

DIY Pizza Party

🕐 **30 minutes**

Create your own pizzeria at home with a DIY Pizza Party! Enjoy endless topping options, crispy crusts, and fun for the whole family.

Ingredients

500g all-purpose flour
7g active dry yeast
1 tsp salt
1 tbsp sugar
300ml warm water
2 tbsp olive oil

Ingredients for Pizza Toppings (suggested):
Tomato sauce
Mozzarella cheese, shredded
Pepperoni slices
Bell pepper slices
Red onion slices
Mushrooms, sliced
Fresh basil leaves
Freshly grated Parmesan cheese
Olive oil
Salt and pepper to taste

Method

- Prepare the Pizza Dough:
- In a large mixing bowl, whisk together the flour, yeast, salt, and sugar.
- Add the warm water and olive oil to the bowl and mix until a dough forms.
- Turn the dough onto a floured surface and knead for about 5 minutes until smooth and elastic.
- Place the dough back into the bowl, cover with a clean cloth, and let it rest and rise for about 1 hour, or until doubled in size.
- Set up Pizza Toppings:
- While the dough is rising, prepare the pizza toppings of your choice. You can provide a variety of options, such as tomato sauce, shredded cheese, sliced vegetables, meat, and herbs, for your guests to choose from.
- Arrange the toppings in separate bowls or plates, along with any sauces, cheeses, or seasonings.

Method

- Preheat the Oven:
- Preheat your oven to the highest temperature possible, typically around 230°C (450°F). If using a pizza stone or pizza steel, place it in the oven to preheat as well.
- Shape the Pizza Dough:
- Once the dough has doubled in size, punch it down to release the air and turn it onto a floured surface.
- Divide the dough into smaller portions, depending on the desired size of the pizzas.
- Using your hands or a rolling pin, shape each dough portion into a round or rectangular shape, about 1/4-inch thick.
- Assemble the Pizzas:
- Transfer the shaped pizza dough to a pizza peel or a parchment-lined baking sheet, if using a pizza stone or pizza steel.
- Let each guest customize their own pizza by adding their preferred toppings onto the dough. Encourage creativity and experimentation with different combinations of flavours and textures.
- Drizzle olive oil over the toppings and sprinkle with salt and pepper to taste.
- Bake the Pizzas:
- Carefully transfer the pizzas onto the preheated pizza stone or pizza steel, if using, or place the baking sheet in the preheated oven.
- Bake for about 10-12 minutes, or until the crust is golden and the cheese is melted and bubbly.
- Serve and Enjoy!
- Remove the pizzas from the oven and let them cool for a few minutes before slicing.
- Serve the hot, freshly baked pizzas and enjoy your DIY Pizza Party with friends and family!

*Note: You can also provide gluten-free or whole wheat dough options for guests with dietary preferences or restrictions. Don't forget to provide plenty of napkins and utensils for everyone to enjoy their delicious homemade pizzas!

Bake-Off Brownies

🕐 **30 minutes**

These Bake-Off Brownies are rich, fudgy, and packed with chocolatey goodness. They're sure to be a hit with anyone who loves a decadent dessert.

Ingredients

1 cup (225g) unsalted butter
2 cups (400g) granulated sugar
4 large eggs
1 tsp vanilla extract
1/2 cup (60g) all-purpose flour
1/3 cup (30g) cocoa powder
1/4 tsp salt
1/2 cup (90g) chocolate chips or chunks

Method

- Preheat the Oven:
- Preheat your oven to 180°C (350°F) and grease a 9x13-inch baking pan.
- Melt the Butter:
- In a microwave-safe bowl or a saucepan, melt the butter until fully melted and smooth.
- Mix the Wet Ingredients:
- In a large mixing bowl, whisk together the melted butter and granulated sugar until well combined.
- Add the eggs one at a time, whisking well after each addition.
- Stir in the vanilla extract.
- Add the Dry Ingredients:
- Sift the flour, cocoa powder, and salt into the bowl with the wet ingredients.
- Stir gently with a spatula or whisk until just combined, being careful not to overmix.
- Fold in the chocolate chips or chunks.

Method

- Bake the Brownies:
- Pour the brownie batter into the prepared baking pan and spread it evenly.
- Bake in the preheated oven for 20-25 minutes, or until a toothpick inserted into the center of the brownies comes out with a few moist crumbs.
- Be careful not to overbake, as the brownies should be fudgy and moist in the center.
- Cool and Cut:
- Remove the brownies from the oven and let them cool completely in the pan on a wire rack.
- Once cooled, cut into squares or rectangles to serve.
- Optional: Add Toppings (if desired):
- You can dust the brownies with powdered sugar, drizzle with melted chocolate, or top with nuts, sprinkles, or other toppings of your choice to add extra flair to your bake-off brownies.
- Serve and Enjoy:
- Serve the delicious bake-off brownies to your friends, family, or bake-off competitors, and enjoy the rich, fudgy, and chocolatey treat!

Note: You can also add other mix-ins to the brownie batter, such as nuts, dried fruits, or even swirl in some peanut butter or Nutella for added flavor and texture. Get creative and have fun with your bake-off brownies!

Conclusion

Thank you for hopping aboard the Baking Express!

I am thrilled to have shared my favourite recipes with fellow baking enthusiasts. Baking has been my passion since a young age, and I am excited to inspire and empower others to discover the joy of creating delicious treats in the kitchen.

Each recipe has been carefully curated to showcase a variety of flavours and techniques, with plenty of room for personal creativity and experimentation.

I also share tips and tricks that I have learned throughout my baking journey, with the hope of helping readers improve their skills and confidence in the kitchen. Thank you for joining me on this sweet adventure, and happy baking!

Quick Reference

Introduction | Welcome Aboard the Baking Express!

Speedy Sweets
Quick and Easy Cookies

Marvelous Muffins
Fast and Flavourful Bites for Breakfast

Brownie Bonanza
Quick Fixes for Chocolate Cravings

Instant Indulgence
No-Bake Desserts for Every Occasion

Cake in a Flash
Simple and Scrumptious Single-Layer Cakes

Cupcake Craze
Quick Tips for Creative Cupcake Decorating

Quick Bread Bliss
Savoury and Sweet Loaves to Love

Speedy Snack Bars
Nutritious Baked Bites for On-the-Go Teens

Pancakes and Waffles
Fast and Fabulous Breakfast Treats

Time-Saving Tips
Baking Hacks for Busy Teen Bakers

Make-Ahead Magic
Prepping Your Ingredients for Stress-Free Baking

Baking with Friends
Fun Group Baking Activities and Challenges

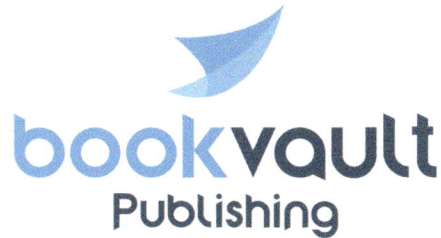

bookvault
Publishing

Baking Express: Quick & Delicious Treats for Busy Teens

ISBN: 9781804674307
Perfect Bound

First published in 2023 by bookvault Publishing, Peterborough, United Kingdom

An Environmentally friendly book printed and bound in England by bookvault, powered by printondemand-worldwide

9781804674307

BVRSH - #0006 - 281123 - C156 - 297/210/11 - PB - 9781804674307 - Matt Lamination